The Spirited Scarecrow

Halloween Madness - Book 3
A Starlight Investigation Short Story

Marnie Atwell

ISBN: 978-0-6483158-4-1

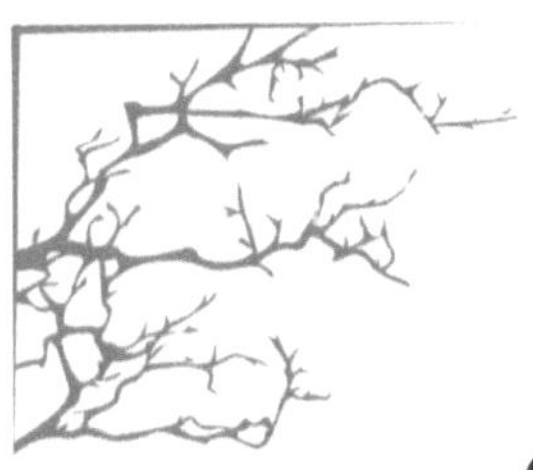

Chapter One

It hurt to breathe. Her chest ached as she tried to drag enough air into her lungs to fill the void. She stood doubled over, a fist shoved into her mouth to quieten the sound of her ragged breathing. Tears streamed from her eyes as she listened intently for any sound that would indicate his whereabouts.

She knew she couldn't stay there, but was too frightened to move. *'If you don't keep moving, he'll find you,'* she repeated in her head as she tried to gather enough courage to place one foot in front of the other. She detected the crunch of dried grass underfoot. The sound came from behind her and slightly to the right. Her body gave a jolt, and her feet began to propel her body forward.

"You can't stay hidden forever, fairy. I *will* find you."

'Why are you doing this to me?' she wondered. Because he could, she realised.

A sob escaped her throat as she blundered through the cornfield. She wished she could fly above the vegetation, but that would make it easier for him to spot her. Keeping to ground level, she had no way of knowing how far she was from the garden's edge. "I am not going to die today," she whispered as she hovered a few centimetres above the dirt.

His footfalls became simpler to pinpoint as he took less care in keeping his location a secret. Briella came to the realisation he was messing with her head as he hunted her. He wanted her to know where he was. She wasn't sure why, though she knew there must be a reason for his sudden change in strategy. *I must be close to safety,'* she thought. *'We must be nearing an area where he can't follow me.'*

A stretch of light appeared in front of her, increasing her feelings of hope. She dug deep into her reserves of energy to increase her speed towards the sanctuary. A giggle of relief escaped her as she realised how close she was to evading his clutches. She reached out with her hands, her eyes glistening as the rays of light touched her fingertips. "Ah," she gasped as it caressed her skin.

"Freedom!" she yelled happily, moments before being scooped up by a gloved hand. "No," she cried, kicking her legs and using her hands to try to pry herself free. She was brought up to face height of her captor and found herself staring into his strange orange eyes.

"I've got you now," he grinned, bringing her even closer.

"No!" Briella screamed, launching herself into a sitting position. Her breathing was ragged, and her heart was racing. She glanced around the room, taking in her surroundings. She was in April's room at the pub, safe and sound. Briella breathed a sigh of relief. "It was just a dream."

She fluttered off the bed and flew to the window, testing the frame to see if it was locked. It opened easily, giving her access to the roof. Briella flew to the peak and sat on the ridge, soaking up the moonbeams. She closed her eyes and took a deep breath, becoming startled when Scout appeared out of nowhere and spoke to her. "Can't sleep?"

With her hand resting over her heart, Briella answered, "No."

"Something on your mind?"

"Just a bad dream. I couldn't get back to sleep so I thought I'd come out here to re-energise."

Scout sat on the corrugated iron and threw an arm over Briella's shoulder. "Your dream wouldn't have anything to do with a scarecrow, would it?"

Briella scoffed. "As if."

"We don't need to make one, you know. I thought it might be a good experiment, but not if it is going to make you lose sleep."

"Why would a scarecrow make me lose sleep? They are designed to scare crows away from the farmer's crops. They are not real, Scout."

"I know that, and yet the mere mention of the name has your hand shaking so hard you could sprinkle glitter over an A4 piece of paper and reach all the edges."

"I'm sorry, Scout. I know it's illogical to be frightened of scarecrows, but I can't help it."

"Phobias aren't logical, Briella, and knowing that doesn't make them any less scary. The only way to combat a phobia is to face it head on, with the support of your family and friends."

"I am not creating a scarecrow and bringing it to life, Scout."

"I am no longer asking you to. I wouldn't have in the first place if I'd known how it was going to affect you. What would help you feel more settled?"

"Maybe doing some more sketches. I could draw some jack-o-lanterns that look similar to the guys at the pumpkin patch. At least then, I would be able to control their actions."

"Wouldn't it be better to stop thinking about Halloween altogether?"

"Don't be silly, Scout. We don't have a lot of time to finish our preparations for the party."

"If you think that will make you feel better," Scout said with a doubtful tone. She scrunched up her face in thought. "Would the jack-o-lanterns you draw be able to give off light like the carved ones do when you light the candle inside?"

"I don't know. I suppose they would be pretty useless if they didn't."

"They wouldn't be useless, Briella."

"Of course they would. You wouldn't be able to see them, and what would be the point?"

"How about you draw one and we'll test it out. If they are able to shine some light, you can draw some more to your heart's content. If not, then you know to spend your time drawing other props. Do you think we need more, considering the party will probably be held in the House of Horrors?"

"Absolutely. There will be people partying outside as well. They won't want to spend all their time inside the house."

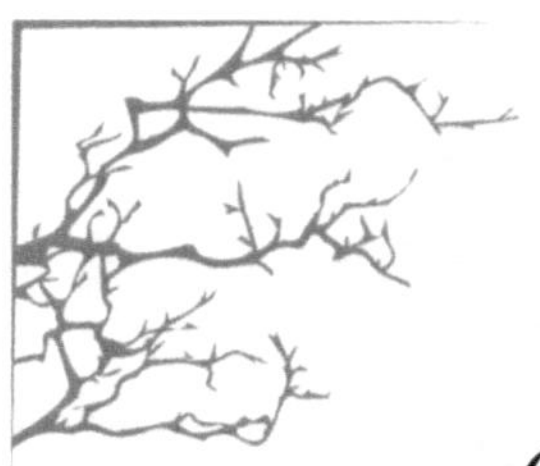

Chapter Two

Scout and Briella made their way to the art studio where Briella's pencils and sketchpad lay waiting. Rather than risk waking April, who was getting in a couple of hours sleep, Scout put some of her fairy dust into a spare lantern to light the workspace.

"Ooh, I like this one, too," Briella gushed quietly, admiring the glow of the crescent-shaped moon.

"I prefer the star one myself," Scout admitted, picturing the way the fire had shimmered as they'd made their way through the carpark to test a picture of a house Briella had drawn. The star appeared to sparkle, bringing a smile to her face.

"Both the lanterns are beautiful, aren't they?" Briella said, not expecting an answer as she opened the sketchpad to a blank page and began the outline of a pumpkin. "Do you think it would be bad to capture John's likeness in the picture?"

Scout placed her hand on Briella's shoulder. "He would be honoured."

"Do you really think so?" Briella asked, searching Scout's eyes for the truth of her words.

"I'm sure if he was still animated by your magic, he would tell you that himself."

April's voice came softly from the bed, "If he were still here, Briella wouldn't need to draw him, would she?"

"Sorry to wake you, April," Briella said, her voice being heard through April's mind-linking ability. "I forgot to lock down my thoughts."

"Doesn't matter, Love. I've had enough sleep to last me another week. Can I get you anything, girls?" April swung her legs over the edge and rose to a sitting position.

"No thanks," they answered, returning their attention to the sketchpad.

April stood up and walked to the bathroom. After using the facilities, she swapped her pyjamas for a tank top and pair of shorts. Grabbing a hair-tie off the surface of the vanity, she placed her long, caramel coloured hair into a high ponytail. "Then I'll leave you to it," April replied, heading for her running shoes sitting by the door. She slipped them onto her feet and quietly closed the door behind her as she left.

April loved this time of the day. It was just over an hour until dawn, and the air was the coolest it was going to be for the rest of the day. Although her feet stepped lightly and barely made a sound, she was nearly knocked off her feet by a red and white husky. A scowl tried to take over her face as her mouth opened to let out the laugh that was making its way up her respiratory system.

The resulting strangled sound nearly had her tripping over her feet in embarrassment.

"Dammit, Liam! You are going to get us kicked out of here," she hissed, glancing around but not seeing anybody. *'Whoever's on reception duty must be in the loo,'* she thought, knowing the counter wouldn't be vacant for long.

"Not me, Honey. Just you," he smirked, transforming to his human state.

"You'll be joining me if someone notices your irises. Honestly, Liam. How have you not been caught?" She narrowed her eyes at his guilty expression. "You were discovered, and yet you still haven't learnt your lesson." She clenched her fist to stop herself from smacking him on the back of the head. "What did you do, manipulate their memories?"

"Would you rather they knew of our existence?" he asked, taking her elbow in his gentle grip and leading her towards the exit.

"I would prefer you kept your eyes that gorgeous shade of chocolate like you had before they irradiated us, and caused them to turn coral."

"Why do you always resort to feelings of violence when you are unhappy with me?" he muttered, registering the tension in her body.

"I have no idea," she blurted before thinking. He turned to look at her but was thwarted when she averted her face. He stopped walking, tugging on her arm so that she did the same.

"Look at me, April."

"Dawn will be here soon. I want to get my run in before it gets too hot," she looked slightly to the left, avoiding direct contact with his eyes.

Force furrowed his eyebrows as he tried to figure out April's behaviour. She was acting weirdly, but he couldn't work out why. He felt terrible that he had made her angry again. His eyes deepened in colour until they appeared normal. "Would you prefer to run on your own?"

She turned to tell him that was precisely what she wanted, but sighed when her eyes met his. "No," she said instead.

His face lit up with a grin, causing her heart to skip a beat. He moved towards the door, his hand sliding from her elbow to grip her hand. "Why don't we make this interesting?"

"What did you have in mind?" April turned to face him head-on. She eased herself from his grip and folded her arms. Force chuckled quietly. "Trying to intimidate me, Love?"

"No, and what's with this sudden need to call me love all the time?"

"I had a dream," he said with a wiggle of his eyebrows.

"Hmmm, going to leave that one alone," April huffed, grabbing the handle of the door and pushing it open.

"Chicken?"

"Of you?" she scoffed. "Hardly."

"Okay then, how about a race to our new house and back. Winner buys the loser breakfast."

"Seriously. You can do better than that."

"Um, that is a bit lame, isn't it? If I win, you spend a day in the bush with me."

"If I win, you spend a day at the beach with me," she grinned, knowing she wasn't as averse to a day in the woods as he was to spend a day on the sand.

"Deal," he agreed, holding out his hand.

April placed her hand in his, and they shook on it. "I need to warm up first. Twice around the pub should do it. What do you think?"

"Yeah, that should be enough to limber up."

April began her first lap. Force couldn't help himself. His eyes went straight to her rear end. "I'm not going to win if I'm behind her," he muttered, moving his feet and picking up his pace. "Too nice a distraction," he said as he passed her

April laughed. Nothing had changed. That was the way she always won. Start off quicker than him, and he would forget they were racing each other. She hadn't had a chance to spend much time in the surf when she and Scout made the trip to the coast. How lovely it would be to see Force in a pair of board shorts, surrounded by women, and not being able to appreciate it because of the irritating feeling of sand in his pants.

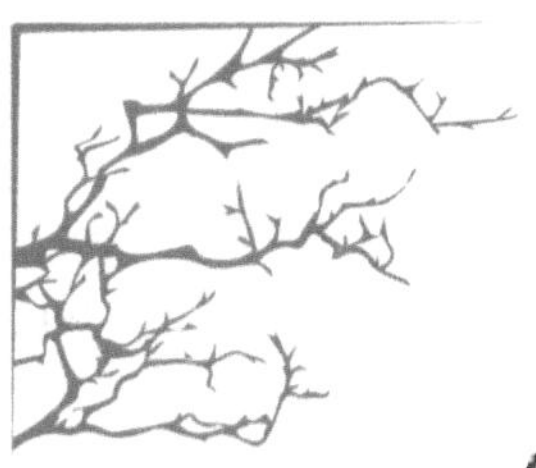

Chapter Three

April let him have the lead during the warm-up round. She enjoyed the view as much as he did, though she never allowed herself to become distracted from the prize, winning. His buns were sweet to look at, but the rippling effect of his back muscles as he swung his arms when in full motion was magnificent. Something she wouldn't get to enjoy this morning if she wanted to win.

Even at this time of the day, the humidity was enough to ensure the sweat clung to her skin. April wasn't particularly fond of that feeling, though she wasn't interested in asking her superiors for a transfer either. She did love the burning sensation in her muscles after a good workout and the shower afterwards compensated for any discomfort that came with the weather.

"Keeping up back there?" Force called over his shoulder. April ignored him but made sure she was looking somewhere other than him in case he could see her admiring his physique. Force finished the lap and lengthened his stride. He turned to face her, running backwards. "What's the matter, don't have enough oomph to speak? Conserving your energy won't make any difference to the outcome, you know."

April smiled, barely puffing for air. "Well then, I suppose I had better say something so you can't use that as an excuse when I beat you to the finish line."

"Oh, you're going down, Lane."

"Ooh, using my surname, Liam. I'm shaking in my boots."

Force croaked with laughter. "You're not wearing any." He turned around and picked up his pace. "You're going down when we hit that start line, Sunshine."

"Bring it!" she returned.

Force slowed his gait to ensure they crossed the line simultaneously. With a final smirk in her direction, he lengthened his stride and broke slightly ahead. April wasn't the least bit concerned. They had done this on many occasions, to the point where she could practically count down to the point when he would turn around to see how far behind she was. Until that point was reached, she concentrated on her breathing and gauging the distance to the cottage that would soon be theirs.

April wasn't sure how she felt about the place. Her mood kept flipping whenever she thought about it. One moment she was happy thinking about chilling in the country, the next she was terrified she would become bored after a couple of days. She had only managed to keep it together during her recent stay as she was busy creating a two storey masterpiece for Scout to live in full-time, and Briella to stay at during her holidays.

Now that the rooms had been constructed, there was nothing to occupy her time and keep her mind busy. The assembly of the home would only take a couple of hours once the settlement was finalised. She wasn't the gardening type and had already decided she would leave the landscaping to Liam.

When she glanced at him, she realised her thoughts had slowed her quite considerably. When he turned around to determine her position, he had to manoeuvre himself further than expected. This led him to land on the ground in a tangled heap. Laughter burst from April as she approached him. She launched herself into the air, her legs scissoring as she hurdled his body. She would have made it had he not lifted his hand and taken hold of her ankle.

April came down hard, forcing the air from Force's diaphragm as her knee was driven into his torso. She heard a grunt before her head hit the hardened earth of the meadow. Her vision blurred from the tears welling in her eyes and her arm rested at an awkward, abnormal angle.

"Liam," she groaned, holding back the sobs that threatened to take control.

Force lay on his side with bent legs, gripping his hands to his chest as he struggled to take a breath. Until he could fill his lungs with oxygen, he would be of no use to his friend. He stretched his arm until his hand rested on her thigh. It was the best he could do under the circumstances. Finally, after what seemed like an eternity, his chest began to expand.

After a few minutes, it became clear to him that some of his ribs were broken. His breathing was ragged, and the act was excruciatingly painful. Regardless of this fact, Force crawled to his knees and bent over April's body. He placed his hands over her arm, closing his eyes against her moans of pain as he mended her broken elbow, and healed the torn ligaments in her wrist. He shuffled further up her body and placed his hand on her forehead. Healing energy soon had the lengthy lacerations and bruises fading away. Pulsing his energy deeper, he ensured she wouldn't suffer any ill effects from a concussion.

He collapsed on top of her, slipping into unconsciousness from the pain. April wriggled until she was no longer pinned by his body. Her eyes quickly scanned his body to determine his injuries. The first thing she noticed was the lack of movement in his chest area. She tenderly touched his shoulder blades, allowing their energies to mix. Within seconds, she discovered his broken ribs and collapsed lung and began rectifying the problem. Once the damage was fixed and he was breathing again, she rested on her haunches, before rubbing her forearm across her face to remove the sweat that had accumulated.

Force rolled onto his back and smiled at her. "I would have fully healed in a couple of hours."

"I would have too, but you chose to heal me."

"You were about to wail with despair," he rose to a sitting position, his eyebrows cocked. "I couldn't have that now, could I?"

"I was not about to cry like a baby," she growled, springing to her feet and placing her hands on her hips.

"Were too," he scrambled to his feet, mimicking her.

The scowl on her face would have frightened anyone else. He found it amusing. "You know, you really are quite lovely when you are angry," he stated, seeing her in a new light. "Your eyes are beautiful, mesmerising." He stepped closer, lifting a hand to tuck her hair behind her ear. He gazed into her eyes, leaning forward. April felt herself getting caught up in the moment. She watched his advance and wondered what it would be like to be kissed by him. He was almost there when she heard herself say, "Don't!"

Force froze. "Don't what?"

"Don't kiss me," she whispered.

He pulled back and ran his hand through his hair. The length of the prickles on top of his head felt a bit long. *'Need a haircut,'* he thought, but said, "Want to finish the race or head back to the pub?"

April wasn't sure what to do. They had gone from a light hearted, friendly competition to an intensely emotional situation that she didn't know how to deal with. There were so few Gatherers on Earth, only a handful located in Australia. She couldn't afford to take the risk of losing one of the few friends she had. Or could she?

Three thousand years was a long time to be alone. Rochelle had been dating Toren for nearly five hundred years before he was taken from her. Most human relationships were lucky to reach fifty years. That was why the Golden Anniversary was such a big deal in their lifetime. Gatherers were practically immortal, which would create an eternity of awkwardness if the relationship went pear-shaped. She had always been attracted to Liam but had managed to keep their relationship platonic. Apparently, this was something that she needed to spend more time thinking about.

"We should head back," she decided. "Breakfast is on me."

"You would have won if I hadn't knocked you off your feet. Name the day, and I'll clear my schedule."

"Technically, you plucked me from the air, Liam. Anything could have happened between here and the finish line. Why don't we have a rematch?"

"Fine," he stated, turning them around and heading back to their rooms. He grabbed her hand and held it lightly in his own. Her body stiffened as she glanced down. "We've done this many times before, April. I'm sorry I wanted to kiss you. Nothing has to change between us. We can be the same as we were before. I won't overstep the boundary again. You have my word."

She wondered why that comment left a hole in the pit of her stomach.

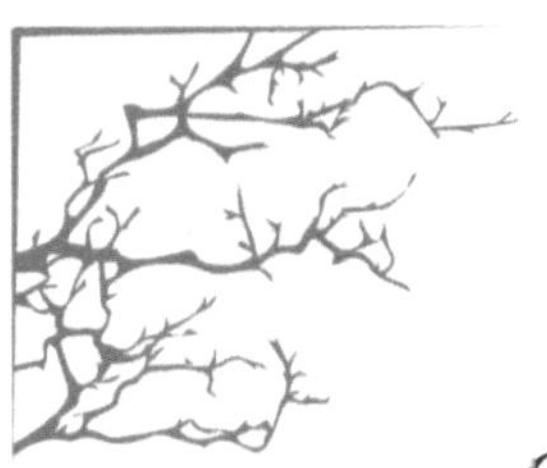

Chapter Four

Briella began sketching the pumpkin patch as it had been before the pumpkins were animated by her magic. She drew the shelter that she and Scout had hidden beneath during the wild storm that had assaulted the town. Briella extended the scene to include the vegetable patch to the east and the cornfield to the north-east.

Scout wondered why Briella was going to such lengths when the purpose of the activity was to see if the jack-o-lanterns she drew would be as perfect for the party as the real pumpkins she'd brought to life. She understood Briella's creative streak could take her in unexpected directions at times, but she hadn't been displaying the traits that would indicate that mood was currently upon her.

Scout glanced at Briella's face and started at what she saw. Instead of the intense concentration that was usually plastered across her face, she saw a vacant look in her eyes and a relaxed jaw. The pencil glided across the page with confident strokes, but it was as though Briella was being used as a puppet. "Briella, are you all right?"

"Hmmm?" she received as an answer.

Scout placed her hand on Briella's shoulder. "Brie, look at me for a minute," she commanded in a soft, yet authoritative tone. Briella ignored her, adding a murder of crows circling high above the ears of corn. When she started drawing poles fit for a scarecrow, Scout really became distressed and reached for her phone.

"What's up Scout?" she heard through the speaker

"Force, come quickly. I think Briella's being possessed by a demon."

"Say again?" he asked, placing her on speaker phone so April could listen in.

"Briella is drawing things and not responding to me at all."

"What things, Scout?" April questioned.

"I think she is about to draw a scarecrow."

April nodded her head in understanding. "Do you know what is going on?" Force asked for Scout's benefit.

"Have you and Briella been talking about scarecrows, Scout?"

"Yeah. I thought she might like to make one. I didn't know she was frightened of them at the time."

"When Briella becomes overtired, she has difficulty in keeping her fears at bay. She tends to go into a fugue state where her mind is able to rest, but her imagination takes over, putting her into a sleep-walk kind of situation. Once she finishes her sketch, she will either fall into a proper sleep or fully awaken. Either way, we need to make her face her fear of scarecrows or her condition will continue to worsen."

"Has this happened before?" Scout inquired.

"Yes, when she watched the movie, *IT*, based on the Stephen King novel. Briella was scared of clowns for months. I thought her fixation was going to kill her."

"We'll get her through this, April," Force said.

"We sure will," Scout agreed, hanging up the phone to monitor her friend. April and Force arrived ten minutes later to find Briella sound asleep on the floor, snuggled beneath her bedspread. "I couldn't fly her to bed. She is too heavy for me to carry over that distance."

"You didn't think to sprinkle her with magic?" Force asked.

"Don't be silly, Liam. What Scout did for Briella was perfectly acceptable," April stated defensively.

"Of course it was," he shook his head. "I didn't mean to imply Scout had been negligent in her duty of care."

April rolled her eyes. "Seriously, Liam. You need to work on your people skills."

Force pursed his lips as he headed for the door. Time to go to his room. "Kids are so much easier to deal with than adults," he muttered under his breath.

"I heard that, Liam."

Force closed his eyes and sighed. *'She's punishing you for wanting to kiss her and changing the rules of the relationship. Don't take her comments to heart.'* he thought. "Later," he called over his shoulder.

"Did something happen while you were gone, April?" Scout asked with a perplexed expression on her face.

"Why do you ask?" April hedged.

"Your energies are mixed up."

"What do you mean?"

"It looks like part of your energy is attempting to integrate with Force and part of his is trying to assimilate into yours. I can see it swirling, looking for a way to connect."

"We had an incident on our run this morning, and we both got hurt. Liam and I healed one another. There must have been some residual energy left over. It will dissipate in time."

"How much time?"

"It depends on how much energy we are talking about. I didn't think I had expended so much that there would be residual energy," April frowned, walking towards the kitchenette. "That would explain why Liam and I were drawn to one another," she mumbled. "As soon as the energy wanes, our feelings should return to normal."

"What was that?" Scout asked, fluttering behind her.

"Nothing," April smiled, turning to face her. "Can I get you some nectar?"

"That would be lovely," Scout answered. "How are we going to tackle the scarecrow thing?"

"Firstly, I am going to give Briella a makeover. Her red and black ensemble is not conducive to facing and letting go of her fear. I think a lovely combination of yellow and pink will be bright enough to wash away the terrors that lie deep within her."

"Can I watch? I've seen the results of your beauty sessions and would really love to see the processes that take place to make that happen."

"Of course, Scout. I have a surprise for you that you might like. Or not," she shrugged. "I guess we'll find out, won't we?"

"What is it?"

"Part of your witch costume for the party. It is Briella's idea. Come, and I'll show it to you."

April grabbed a blossom from the bottom cupboard and handed it to Scout. She led her to a section of the fairies' new house that would become Scout's bedroom and opened the door of the wardrobe. Inside, on a hanger, was a set of plum coloured hair extensions. "I thought you might like to try these. I believe it will look nice with your new witch's hat."

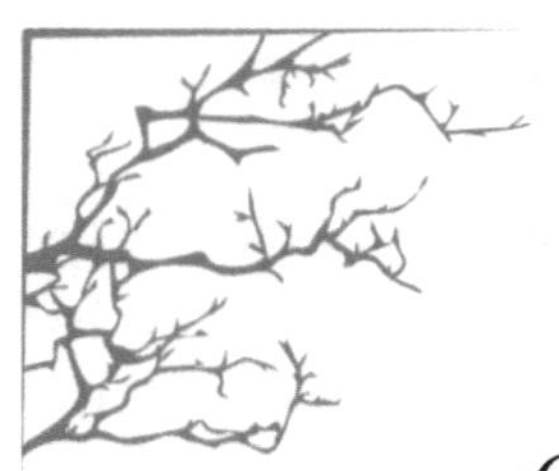

Chapter Five

April detected the feelings of apprehension that swirled in Scout's mind. She placed the hanger back in the wardrobe and said, "Maybe some other time."

Scout felt terrible. April had been cautiously excited to show Scout her latest labour of love. She noticed the flash of disappointment that crossed April's face before she could hide her feelings from view. It was only for a moment, but it was long enough to make Scout suck up her fear of change, and to allow April to introduce her to something new.

"Take that back out, please April. Show me how it'll look."

"Are you sure, Scout? It is not a permanent change but it will take me about thirty minutes to weave into your existing strands."

"How long will it last for?"

"As long as you want. I can take it out whenever you like."

"I've got nothing else to do. There are no monsters on the radar and Briella is asleep. How about you?"

"I wouldn't have shown you if I didn't have time to do it now. There is no way I would give you time to think about something like this. You would talk yourself out of it before you gave it a chance."

Scout laughed, "I can't get over how well you know me."

"You are not hard to read, Scout. Your feelings might be complex, but you like to keep things simple. No surprises."

Scout harrumphed. She'd always thought of herself as a complicated creature. It was a kick in the guts to realise she was actually quite simple to read. "Where do you want me?"

"Over there," she pointed to the bench separating the kitchenette from the living area. April collected a bar stool from another section of Scout's new house. It was carved from wood with a green leafed cushion tied to the seat for comfort and a high back to support the upper body

She placed the chair on the laminated surface and placed a magnifying glass in front. "Sit with your front resting against the back of the chair, Scout. That will give me easier access and allow the hair extensions to fall naturally."

Scout did as asked and took a couple of calming breaths. She could feel the tension in her body and with a few reassuring words to herself, felt her body relax.

"That's great, Scout. This shouldn't hurt, but if you feel me pulling a little too tightly on your strands of hair, don't be afraid to let me know. I would like this to be a pleasurable experience for you."

Scout couldn't see that happening. She didn't enjoy being touched by another, so couldn't understand how someone playing with her hair could be considered pleasurable. Scout was pleasantly surprised. April had a gentle touch, and it was almost relaxing having her massage the strands of hair before threading the tip of the extension and weaving it in. Although Scout's sleep had been restful and restorative, she felt her eyelids begin to droop.

"You okay, Scout?" April asked.

"Yeah. Feeling a little sleepy," she answered in a surprised tone.

April merely smiled, feeling immensely pleased with herself. Knowing people, and fairies, better than they knew themselves was one of her many talents. While Scout was under the assumption she was happiest when she was alone, April knew that deep down she craved small doses of intimate interactions with others. A conversation that only occurs between two close friends. A hug of friendship. A burst of laughter so intense, it causes pain in the abdominal region. A person who is willing to give up half an hour of their day in the pursuit of making another feel happy, as April was doing for Scout.

"Talk to me so I can stay awake," Scout said tiredly.

"What do you want to talk about?"

"How often are you and Briella going to come and stay?"

"I don't know," April confessed. "The staff at Starlight Investigations feel we have already overstayed our welcome. They are happy with us making day trips to chill out together, but don't want us having extended visits."

"How did Rochelle and Toren manage their relationship?"

"When they weren't working on a case, they made sure the time they had together wasn't wasted on frivolous things."

"Like what?"

"Sitting around all day watching the television, or playing game consoles. They lived in the minute and for each other. It didn't hurt that Toranthian had a friend who owned a helicopter. He spent a lot of time flying them from one area to the next so they could ensure they weren't shirking their duties to the humans for their own pursuits."

"Why don't you have a boyfriend, April?"

"We've discussed this before."

"Tell me again," Scout pleaded.

"I am immortal. Humans are not. End of story."

"What about Liam and Callum? A couple of hot guys with gorgeous personalities."

"They are colleagues and off limits."

"Hmmm. That tells me a few things."

"Oh really?"

"Yep. You like one of them but are afraid of taking the first step. What I can't work out is why. Rochelle and Toren were together for five centuries. That is not something that can be kept hidden from the authorities, so I am guessing they turned a blind eye to the relationship. That being the case, why would you not pursue your own happiness with one of the Gatherers?"

"I do not wish to pursue a relationship with Liam or Callum. I am not afraid of what the Starlight Investigations team or our Queen has to say on my choice of partner. I have simply not met anyone I like enough to take the risk of getting hurt."

"That's a lie, but I'll let it go. It is none of my business anyway, whether or not you are dating. You are a beautiful woman, April, both inside and out. I'd like to see you happy."

"I am happy. I don't need a relationship to complete me."

"That is not what I meant," Scout said defensively.

"I love my life, Scout. Be assured that I am content and wouldn't change a thing. There, I'm done. Come, take a look."

April picked up a compact that lay to her right. She opened it to reveal a mirror under the lid and foundation in the base. Pointing the mirror towards Scout, April waited anxiously for her reaction. The look on her face was priceless.

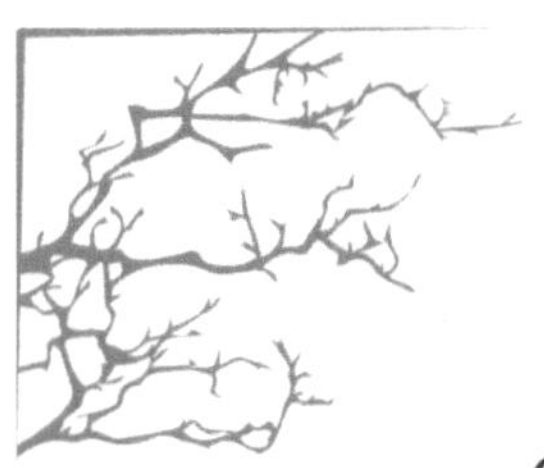

Chapter Six

"April?" Briella's voice broke through April's thoughts. She glanced over to the studio and saw Briella stirring beneath the covers. She placed the compact on the benchtop, "Briella's awake. I'll leave you in peace to admire my handiwork."

Scout barely acknowledged her words. She was astounded by the change in her appearance. She appeared to have lost years off her age, and her face seemed even more pensive than usual. April must have put something in her hair to change the colour to match the strands. Gone was the lilac, to be replaced by plum. Scout wasn't sure if she liked the tone or not. It would take a few glances at her reflection before she would be able to decide for sure. It didn't look terrible, just different.

Scout turned around to peer over her shoulder. The locks fell almost to waist length. That would be a problem should she choose to keep them. There were all sorts of things that could get tangled up in her hair. It would be lovely to go for a fly and see what it felt like to have the wind blowing through her hair.

She sometimes glanced at Briella a little wistfully when they were in flight, Briella's hair blowing alluringly behind her, gently brushing her skin. Scout would finally know what that felt like, but wasn't sure the length of the hair suited her. Briella fluttered over for a look and was flabbergasted. "Wow, Scout. You look beautiful."

"Thanks, Briella," she muttered, giving her friend a quick glance before returning her gaze to the mirror. "I'm not sure whether I like it or not."

"Do you have the hat?" Briella turned to April.

April walked to the wardrobe and opened another door. She pulled out the hat and placed it on Scout's head.

"Oh, yeah," Scout said. "I like that," she nodded her head. "I'm beginning to see the picture in your head, April."

"I didn't want to change things too much for you, Scout, so I thought you could wear your usual pants but pair it with a black top in the same style as the one you are wearing."

"You mean the only style she wears; a purple strapless top."

"Yeah," April chuckled, "that one. I also created a black cape for you to wear. It might get cold, later in the night. There are a pair of black boots as well if you are feeling daring."

"Thanks, April. I'll see how I feel on the night." Scout took the hat off and handed it to April. "You'd better put this away. I might wreck the pointy tip."

April did as asked. "Are you ready for your make-over, Briella?"

"I'd never say no to a make-over, April. I thought you wanted me to keep my black hair with red highlights for the cat outfit."

"The black hair would probably be okay. It would help to keep it hidden under the hood with the cat ears I made for you. The red highlights have to go. None of the cats I've seen has red fur."

"I don't have to look exactly like a cat."

"No, you don't. I thought you might like something brighter for a few days. I can give you back this look on the day of the party, or we can skip the make-over until after the party."

"Are you kidding?" Briella fluttered to the stool and made herself comfortable. "Work your magic, April," she grinned. "Are you sticking around, Scout?"

"You bet. I wouldn't miss this for anything."

"It will take a couple of hours," Briella warned.

"I've got nothing better to do," Scout replied.

April grabbed another stool for Scout to sit on. "You might as well have something soft to sit on."

Scout nestled her bottom into the cushion. "These are comfy chairs. Where did you get them from?"

"I have a friend who makes doll's furniture. I pay him extra to pretend he is making furniture for little people that are real. He hasn't disappointed Briella yet."

April grabbed some chemicals from a cosmetic bag Scout hadn't noticed earlier. She studied the vials that

April withdrew but couldn't read the writing on the labels. "What language is that?"

"An ancient one," April replied.

"Which ancient civilisation does it hail from?" Scout rolled her eyes.

"Don't you roll your eyes at me! It is a secret society that is going to remain a secret."

"Whatever," Scout answered. A rumbling noise outside caught her attention. "That sounds like Force's bike," she flew to the window to investigate. His profile came into view for a few seconds before disappearing around the side of the building. "Where do you think he is going?"

"I don't know," April replied more snarly than usual. "I'm not his keeper."

"Is that jealousy I hear? Where do you *think* he is going?"

"I wouldn't know." But she had an inkling he was going over to Loretta's place.

"Maybe he's visiting Calamity. Checking on her recovery from the Jealousy Monsters."

"He did that a couple of days ago. Why would he check on her again?" Briella queried.

Scout stared at April, a smirk wrestling with her lips. "I am sure those feelings will pass when your energy returns to normal."

"What's wrong with your energy?" Briella asked April.

"Nothing, Briella. I'm fine."

"April and Force healed each other," Scout informed her. "They are not quite themselves. A little more energy than was needed was expended, and the pair appears to be experiencing a connection that didn't exist before."

"What sort of connection?" Briella demanded to know.

"A romantic one," Scout insisted. The smirk now blatantly plastered on her face.

"I see," Briella frowned, thinking quietly to herself.

Scout leaned forward and peered at Briella's face. The smirk was replaced by a genuine smile. Briella caught the movement in her peripheral vision and turned her eyes in Scout's direction. "What are you scheming, now?" she whispered.

"You want April and Force to get together, don't you?"

"Sure, but you already knew that. I told you when we were chasing the vampire."

"Callum is coming here to pose as April's husband, Wade. What if we convince him it would be better to pose as Force instead? Force and April are more closely acquainted than Callum and April. Wouldn't it make more sense for the one who knows her best to play the husband?"

"You are right," Briella replied in a louder voice than intended. In her excitement, she had forgotten to block the mind-link.

"Right about what?" April asked.

"This make-over," she blurted, thinking quickly. "I've been feeling a bit stressed lately, and this will help to soothe my nerves."

April took the opening Briella had given her to discuss her aversion to scarecrows. "What's been plaguing your thoughts, Briella?"

"Nothing worth discussing. I've been a bit uptight, that's all."

"Now, Briella. You know what happens when you don't get what's on your mind out in the open. You fixate on things and make yourself sick."

"Nothing is going to make me sick."

"That's what you said after you watched that movie with the clowns."

"That was different," Briella refused to be swayed.

"How?"

Briella wracked her brain for an answer. She couldn't come up with one fast enough. "You've been talking in your sleep," April said, her fingers crossed behind her back for the white lie she told.

Briella tried to swallow the lump that had suddenly appeared in her throat. "I have?"

"Yes," April nodded.

"What have I been saying?" she gulped.

"Something about a scarecrow."

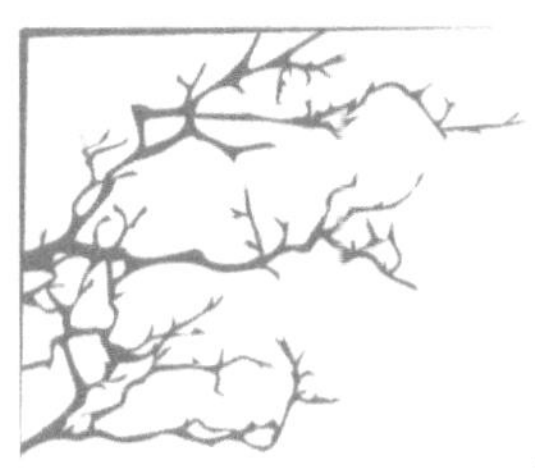

Chapter Seven

Briella's eyes widened, and her knuckles turned white as her fingers tightened on the wood. Scout leaned further forward and placed her hand on Briella's arm. "Tell her."

Briella closed her eyes and lowered her head. April wrapped Briella's hair in plastic and spun the stool, so they were face to face. "What's going on, Briella?" April asked quietly.

Briella looked into her friend's eyes and said, "It's happening again."

April nodded. "Your fear will continue to grow and manifest in ways that are detrimental to your health. With Halloween looming, it is important that we nip this in the bud, NOW. Agreed?"

"Yes," Briella whispered hoarsely.

"It will be okay. We've beaten your fears before. This time will be easier."

"It will? Halloween is going to make it a hundred times worse."

"No, it won't. This time we have Scout and Liam to help, and because of them, you have learned you have some control over the things that happen during the lead up to Halloween."

April moved to another section of Scout's new home and collected a chair similar to those found in hairdressing salons. She also took a couple of containers that had the same appearance as porcelain. One would hold the clean water needed to rinse Briella's hair while the other would store the contaminated water to be disposed of. April placed the chair and collection tank near the girls then moved to the sink.

"So what's your plan?" Briella asked, switching chairs.

"You are going to tell me the items you need to create a scarecrow, and I am going to source them for you. Then we are going to build him to your instructions, and you are going to see there is nothing to be afraid of."

"You forget that one speck of fairy dust and that thing will come alive."

"Yes, but just like the creatures in the drawings were compelled to obey you, I think the scarecrow will be too."

Briella looked sceptical. Scout appeared to mull over April's words. "I can't find fault with that logic." She winked at April. Their plan was going to work. She just knew it. Scout dipped her finger in the water and found it to be lukewarm. "Is that hot enough?" she questioned.

"Yes, Scout. Any hotter and it would stress the roots of the hair and make it fall out."

"I've never seen anyone become bald from having a hot shower," Scout stated.

"It doesn't fall out all at once. But too many hot showers over time will thin out a person's coverage."

"Is that right?" Scout raised her eyebrows. "You are a fountain of knowledge, April. It's a shame we can't keep you."

Briella laughed. "You don't need to keep her, Scout. You will see her all the time."

"Of course, Briella. It's just a manner of speech."

"Right."

"So what does that stuff you put in Briella's hair do? Ooh, can I do that?" Scout watched April rinsing Briella's hair.

"Here you go," April handed Scout a nozzle attached to a hose. "Be sure to keep it out of Briella's eyes," she cautioned. "The chemical removes the colours from Briella's hair leaving it white."

"So it's a bleach, then?"

"Somebody's been watching television."

"Briella might have introduced me to a show or two," Scout admitted sheepishly.

"Mind you don't watch too much. I'd hate to see you become hooked on the soaps."

"Why would I get hooked on soap? I don't even use the stuff when I bathe."

"Not the soap people wash with. Soap Operas, a type of show on television that sees the next story pick up where the last one left off. They can become addictive."

"If you say so. What comes next?" Scout wrapped Briella's hair in a towel. "It feels a bit dry."

"It will feel better once the conditioner goes in, but first, we need to add some colour. I think a nice golden blonde will go nicely with the outfit I have in mind."

April grabbed another vial from the case and opened the lid. She squeezed the dropper and sucked up a bit of the liquid. She added a drop to a white ceramic bowl containing a thick white cream. As she stirred, the colour mixed with the white and the consistency of the cream thinned. April added another drop of colour and stirred. Happy with the result, she applied it to Briella's hair.

"How long does that need to stay on for?"

"Fifteen minutes. While that is working, we will colour Briella's wings."

"How are you going to strip out the red colour? Our wings are very delicate you know."

"Yes, Scout. I know. This isn't my first time doing this."

"Sorry, April." Scout lifted her shoulders and tipped her head to the side.

"It has taken years to perfect the formulae I use on Briella. Please don't try this on your own, Scout. If you want to make some changes, let me know. I'm more than happy to help."

"Don't you like me the way I am?"

"Of course I do, but sometimes a girl just needs a change. If that feeling should ever take hold of you, then I am available to help you do that safely."

"Oh, okay." Scout remained quiet, lost in her own thoughts. April kept a concerned eye on her. She would have to have a word with Liam when he returned. Scout needed a serious boost to her self-esteem. April stripped Briella's wings of the red and added some yellow. Then she rinsed out Briella's hair, adding a sealant and some conditioner. Scout rinsed out the conditioner and then used a blow-dryer for the first time.

"That air gets really hot. How does this thing work?"

"I don't know," April said. "I've never really thought about it, just enjoyed the results."

Briella's hair looked lovely. Scout gathered some fringe strands on the left-hand side and twisted them, pinning them in place. She then repeated the effect on the other side. It was a classic hairstyle for fairies, one that her natural hair was too short to accomplish.

"You look lovely, Briella, but that outfit doesn't go with your hair and wings."

"I have the perfect ensemble for you to wear, Briella," April stated. She collected a pink top that had one button which fastened below her breastbone, long sleeves and yellow tassels. This was complemented with a pair of full-length pants in pink that had a yellow waistband. Yellow high-heeled shoes finished the look.

"How do you feel?" Scout asked once Briella had seen herself in the mirror.

"Like I can take on the world," Briella grinned.

"How about a scarecrow?" April inquired, taking the vessels of water to the sink to dispose of their contents.

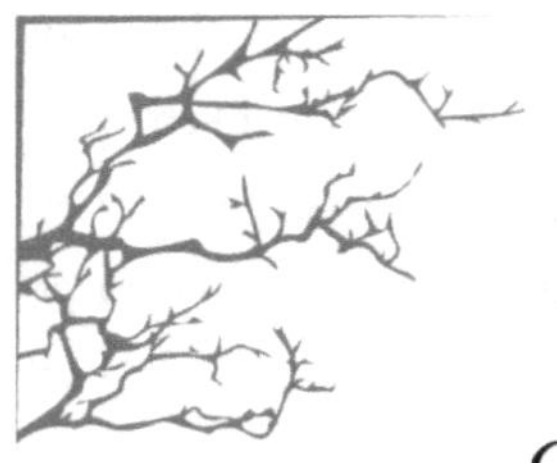

Chapter Eight

S cout noticed Briella's smile fade. "Come on Briella, no need to be scared," she said.

"Yeah, love. Scarecrows are just a bunch of clothes stuffed with straw, designed to scare the birds away from the vegetables. They are inanimate objects that can't hurt you," April said returning to the bench.

"Unless they are infected with my fairy dust."

"Is that what you are afraid of? That it will come to life and terrorise you?" April returned the chairs to their rightful rooms.

"Aren't you?"

"No. So you are not afraid of scarecrows?"

"Yes."

April's mouth twisted to the side. "Yes, as in you *aren't* afraid of scarecrows, or yes, you *are* afraid of scarecrows?"

"Yes, I am afraid of scarecrows."

April and Scout looked at one another. "Are you afraid of a scarecrow being brought to life or any inanimate object coming to life?"

"Both, but the thought of a scarecrow, which absolutely terrifies me, coming to life scares me above all other things."

"You are less afraid of your magic at Halloween this year, than you have been in previous years, right?"

"Yes," Briella agreed.

"That's a start. Let's begin by creating a scarecrow and go from there. Just like with the clowns, we'll take it one step at a time."

"Don't expect me to be all smiles and sunshine."

"I won't," April said gravely.

"Are you taking the Micky out of me?"

"Of course not. I am merely being serious."

"Well don't! It's off-putting."

April raised her eyebrows but was able to prevent the huff that threatened to escape through her lips. "Let's start with his clothes. What is your scarecrow going to wear?"

"A pair of jeans and a t-shirt," Briella blurted, not taking any time to think.

"Okay," April said. "Do you want him to have a hat or shoes?"

"Yeah, sure."

Scout rested her arm across Briella's shoulders and spoke gently. "For this to work you are going to have to take ownership of the decisions for creating him. If you don't want to touch anything for fear of getting your dust on it, that's fine. But you have to be the one who decides what he looks like or you are going to continue being afraid."

"So I won't be afraid of this one, but will still be afraid of the others?" she shrieked.

"No, you won't be scared of any of them if we do this correctly right from the start. What is his body going to be made from?"

Briella actually took the time to think about it. April had said that scarecrows were usually made of straw. There were plenty of ears of corn ready to be harvested on the land they were about to own. Perhaps they could stuff some hessian bags with the stalks to create various parts of the body.

Once they had legs, arms and a torso, April could sew them together. They could use gloves for his hands and toe socks for his feet. These could be filled with rice or sand.

His head could also be constructed from hessian filled with stalks, but would need to be cut to provide holes for the eyes and mouth. April could sew on some ears and a nose made from hessian and filled with rice or sand.

The scarecrow would be bald. Briella didn't want any hair on his head. A hat would have to suffice as a covering.

"So what do you think?" she asked after explaining her ideas to April and Scout.

"Sounds like a plan," Scout answered more quickly than April could open her mouth to voice her thoughts.

Once again, April nodded in reply. "When are we going shopping?"

"*We* are not going shopping. I am. Did you suddenly forget you cannot be seen by humans?"

"We can hide in your purse like every other time we've been out with you," Scout scowled.

"You weren't moving into those areas to live. Humans can take only so many memory scrubs before their brains turn to mush. We need to save those times for when they are truly needed."

"I suppose so," Scout murmured.

"There is no supposing about it, young lady. You are going to have to be more vigilant in keeping your presence on Earth a secret. It is going to be a lot more taxing on your energy levels than you realise." April walked to a counter beside the front door to collect her purse. "What are you going to do while I'm away?"

Briella looked at the clock on the wall. It was too early for her favourite show, '*How Do I Look?*' to come on television. She glanced at Scout, admiring her new look. "We'll find something to amuse ourselves."

"That's what I'm afraid of. I'm not leaving until you tell me what you have in mind."

"I don't see what the big issue is," Briella stamped her foot. "Don't you trust us?"

"Yes, I trust you. You don't trust yourself. You claim you are afraid your dust is going to cause all sorts of trouble and the next minute you are all 'She'll be right mate'. Liam's not here to keep an eye on things."

"No, he's not. Scout is. And she has a phone to call you or Liam if danger comes a-knocking."

"No need to be snarky, Briella. I only have your best interests at heart."

"We'll be okay, April. I'll ensure Briella makes safe choices."

"Thank you, Scout. At least one of you can behave like a grown woman."

"Are you calling me childish?" Briella stamped the other foot.

April didn't bother replying. "I'll be home soon. It shouldn't take long to gather the items we need."

"Take your time," Scout said, pressing her hand firmly over Briella's mouth. Briella's eyes sparkled, catching April's attention. Surely they should appear angry or indignant to have Scout preventing her from letting fly with another inappropriate comment. Instead, they seemed to be jovial, amused even. *What are you up to, Briella?'* April asked through mind-link.

'I thought it would be fun to have a fashion show with Scout as the model. She is rocking the new hairstyle you gave her. I'm not entirely sure how she will respond when I encourage her to play dress-ups with my clothes.'

April's mood lightened. She knew Briella had been hiding something from her. As it turned out, she was protecting her idea from Scout. *'Maybe I had better stay, after all. Scout might get quite upset by your suggestion.'*

'I'm not going to force her, April. There won't be any arguments. If she says no, we'll find something else to do.'

'All right. If you think everything will be okay, I'll leave.'

'Everything is fine, April. Go, have fun. See you when you return.'

"Bye, ladies," April said as she opened the door. "Behave," she reminded them before the door closed behind her.

"Sheesh, I thought she'd never leave," Briella told Scout.

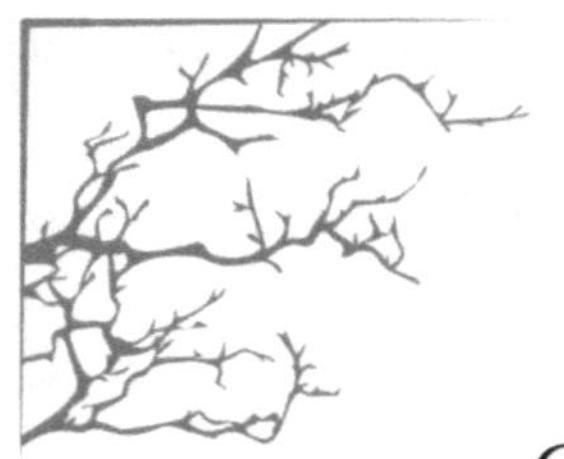

Chapter Nine

Scout had that uh-oh feeling when she looked at the gleam in Briella's eyes. "What are you formulating in that head of yours?" she asked worriedly.

"Nothing that is going to hurt either one of us," Briella answered with a flutter of her wings. "Who knows, Scout? You might even have a little fun."

"I have fun all the time," she huffed defensively.

"I'm not saying you don't," Briella flew to her room and noticed the bedspread was missing. "I'll have to remember to make that," she pointed to the bed before continuing onto her wardrobe. "Now, Scout. I want you to look at the clothes in my cupboard and pick out something that you think will suit your new hairstyle."

"What I have on now looks good."

"I'm sorry to break it to you, Scout, but the colour of your hair and the colour of your top do not go together."

"What do you mean? They are both shades of purple."

"Yes, but the wrong shades to be placed against one another. Perhaps if your pants were that colour and your top was black . . ." Briella's finger had come up to tap her lips while she considered that combination. "No, not even then," she decided.

Scout stood in front of the mirrored side of the wardrobe and studied her reflection with a critical eye. She hated to admit that she agreed with Briella. With a sigh, she said, "I see what you mean."

Briella sidled up beside her, "How about I start you off?" She reached into the cupboard and pulled out the most conservative outfit she owned. Scout eyed the ensemble with appreciative eyes. She had been afraid Briella would push her to wear something that showed too much skin around the waist and too much leg. Instead, she was shown a knee-length skirt in black with a blouse in sky blue that slipped over the head and had off-the-shoulder sleeves.

"When have you worn this?" Scout asked.

"Actually, I haven't had an opportunity to wear that piece yet."

"How long have you had it?" Scout asked, swapping her pants for the skirt, admiring the shape of her calves and the way the bottom flared when she turned.

"A while." When Scout clicked her tongue with annoyance, Briella continued, "I'm not sure exactly. A few years maybe."

"Don't you like it?"

"It's not really my style," she shrugged, waiting impatiently for Scout to put on the shirt. She was surprised at how easy it was to get Scout to try on something new.

"Then why did you get it?" Scout asked, slipping her purple corset over her head and replacing it with the shirt Briella handed her.

"April made it for me when I was going through my Spanish phase. I immersed myself in the language, the dance, the food. I just wasn't into the clothing. It doesn't suit my physique."

Scout disagreed with that comment but kept her thoughts to herself. She thought Briella would look amazing in this outfit. Scout stared at the mirror but wasn't happy with what she saw.

The costume was comfortable but didn't seem to suit the girl in the mirror. Briella stood behind her and fiddled with the fabric. She peered over Scout's shoulder, bunching her hair up in her fist, creating a loose ponytail. "Hmmm, that's better, but I think this outfit calls for curling your hair, allowing it to fall softly over your shoulders."

Scout wasn't comfortable with the way the conversation was going. That seemed like way too much effort to make an outfit look appealing. The clothes she wore needed to look appealing from the moment she put them on. She had more important things to worry about than the way she presented herself to the world.

While these clothes felt lovely, although the skirt was a little breezy, they weren't her. "Do you have anything with pants?"

Briella's grin triggered a shiver to run throughout Scout's body. "Relax," Briella rolled her eyes. "Such little faith."

Scout eyed the outfit and shook her head. "No. Nah-uh. I'm not wearing that."

"Try it on. You might be pleasantly surprised," Briella replied. She held a bodysuit made from lycra in her hands. It was a gorgeous, jungle-green coloured fabric with blocks of black print.

"Where do those words sit?"

"Try it on and see," Briella said mysteriously. Scout humoured her. She knew it would not be to her taste, but this way Briella couldn't come back at her for not being open to new things. Scout chuckled quietly to herself. Who was she kidding? They both knew she wasn't any good with change.

Still, she took the outfit from Briella's outstretched arms after disrobing and wriggled her way inside the stretchy fabric. The colour complimented her new hair tone perfectly. It also highlighted the creaminess of her skin. As expected, the words *Check this out* was written across her chest and the words *Hot or not?* were written across her backside.

Other words were strewn across her abdomen, legs and back. She wasn't as concerned by those. "How many times have you worn this one?" Scout asked.

"Every time Queen Glitter throws a ball and insists I attend."

"I'm guessing that is why I have never seen you at one."

"Yep, she throws me out every time."

"Why don't you want to stay?"

"I'm not interested in starting a family. Here, try this one on." She reached into the wardrobe and pulled out a shirt similar to Scout's corset. It was a deep purple with sparkling swirls rising up like fireworks. Scout's eyes lit up as though it was Christmas. Briella groaned, knowing her fun had come to an end. "I was trying to save this for later," she said.

"Yeah, because you know it's the kind of clothes I like wearing. This is beautiful," Scout breathed. "Why have I never seen you in this?"

"I'm not wearing the same style as you when we are together, and since you never wear anything else . . ."

"Right," Scout said a little tersely.

Briella wasn't about to offer an apology. She understood Scout's desire to be comfortable. It was difficult for her friend when she was placed in a position where she needed to step outside her comfort zone.

It was why Scout spent a lot of time on her own. She was able to do whatever took her fancy, and avoid whatever made her feel uncomfortable.

The thing Scout didn't comprehend, was there were ways of creating new comfort zones, and Briella was determined to teach her that. She was beginning to realise that it was going to take longer to train Scout than she thought.

That was okay. Briella had plenty of time to transition her friend into a fashionista like her.

Scout peeled the bodysuit off and retrieved her black pants. She slid the shirt over her head and allowed it to fall into place. Her gasp when she looked in the mirror brought a tear to Briella's eye.

"Baby steps," Briella murmured quietly.

"Baby steps," Scout reiterated, having read her lips in the mirror.

Briella grabbed a pin from a drawer and drew the sides of Scout's hair back. She pinned it in place and plucked at her fringe hairs. "Perfect," she uttered, admiring her work.

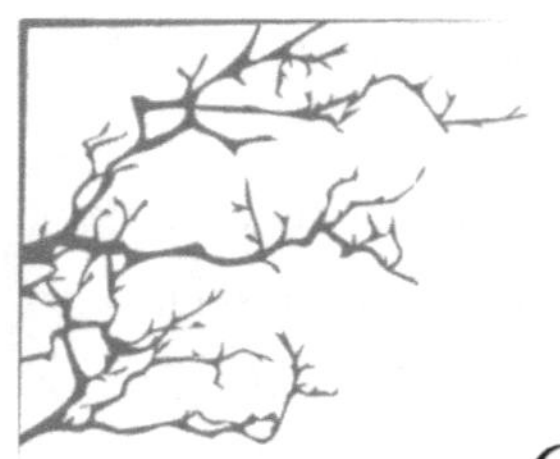

Chapter Ten

The rumble of Force's bike signalled his return. Scout looked panicked as she stepped closer to the mirror. She ran her hand through her hair, nearly jumping out of her skin as Briella shrieked. "Don't do that! You'll mess it up if you continue to pat it." Briella slapped her hand away.

"Do you mind?" Scout shouted back. "You scared me half to death," she puffed the air in and out of her lungs around the words.

"What is up with you anyway?" Briella asked with narrowed eyes.

"Nothing," her head came up as Force entered the room.

"April? Girls?"

"Over here," Scout answered, dropping the barrier to the mind-link.

Force wandered over, his eyes widening at Scout's new look. "Somebody's been busy," he smiled. "You look lovely, Scout."

"Thanks, Force. Where have you been?"

"Out and about," he hedged. "Where's April?"

"Out shopping for scarecrow stuff," Briella answered.

"You're okay with that?" he asked.

"Briella told her what to buy," Scout replied proudly.

"Seems like I've missed a lot. Want to catch me up."

"Sure, but there may not be time," Briella's gaze was drawn to the window. "I believe April has returned. Are you two going to be weird?"

"Why would we be weird?" he wandered to the window, to see her car heading towards the parking area.

"You two did heal each other, right?"

"So?"

"There are ramifications for those who use more energy than is necessary."

"Such as?"

"Romantic feelings," the fairies' voices blasted in stereo.

"Is that right?" Force said, pieces of the puzzle falling into place. "Has April indicated she might be feeling some after-effects of the healing?"

"Nope, you did," Briella laughed. "When you came home and made her mad, again. The look on your face when she responded told us you wanted to smack her or kiss her. Instead, you chose to turn and walk away. Dead giveaway."

"Do you still want to kiss April?" Scout asked, fluttering at eye level.

"No."

"Do you want to think about that? She's about to walk in the door."

Force opened his mouth to speak when the door opened behind him. "I'm home," April called happily. "Wait until you see what I've bought."

The fairies glanced at her shopping bags. They attempted to appear intrigued but failed miserably. As Briella had already stated what she wanted, they already knew what would be in there. Unless, April had bought something on impulse. Scout flew to April, "Did you get something that wasn't on the list, April?"

Her smile said it all. She raised her head and spotted Force. "Liam, I didn't know you had returned. Did you have a good morning?"

"Hmmm, you?"

"For Heaven's sake, you two. Are you seriously going to stand there and make pleasantries?" Scout wiggled her finger at them both. "Work out your feelings and get back to normal. If you are going to be awkward around each other, Force may as well buy out April's share of the house and you and Briella can stay along the coastline."

"There's no need to go that far," Force stated. He didn't want April to leave and not return. He would miss her, terribly. "We are fine, aren't we, love?"

April raised an eyebrow. He'd referred to her as 'love' again. For the sake of the girls she chose to let it slide. "Yes, girls. There is no need for drastic measures. Liam and I were confused by the circulation of the excess energy. Are our auras back to normal?" she asked Scout.

Scout confirmed their energies had stabilised. "Have the energies amalgamated or dissipated?" Force asked.

"Seems like they have dissipated. Your colours are as they were yesterday."

"Great. How about we look inside those shopping bags and get started on our newest project."

"What else did you buy, April?" Briella asked.

"Nothing important," she said, walking behind the divider that separated the sleeping area from the living areas. Depositing a small pink bag in a drawer, she returned to see the three of them rifling through her shopping.

"Like what you see, Briella?" she queried.

"Everything is perfect. Are we going to go and get the stalks from the cornfield and bring it back here for assembly, or should we assemble it there?"

"What would make you feel more comfortable about the whole process?"

Briella thought back to her dream and felt her fear beginning to rise. The thought of having it chase her through the cornfields had sweat springing from the pores on her forehead. "Here," she croaked. "We should put it together, here."

"Him, Briella. Don't think of the scarecrow as *'it'*. He will be less scary if you refer to the scarecrow as *'him'.*"

"Whatever. Can you and Force go and get the stuff to fill the bags with? Scout and I will start filling the feet and hands. Did you get sand or rice?"

"I bought some sandpit sand. Shouldn't one of us stay with the two of you?"

"No. You two need to get your friendship back to normal. You can't do that with us around."

Force reached for April's hand. He held it in his for a few seconds before letting go. "Anything?"

"Nope," April answered. "You?"

"Nope."

"All right then, we'll be off," April stated. "Oh, and Scout, I love the top you are wearing and the way you've done your hair."

"Thanks, April."

"We'll be back soon," Force said, leading April towards the door.

"Okay," the girls cried, gathering some implements to transport the sand from the bag to the gloves and socks.

When the door closed behind the Gatherers, Briella said, "So, they're really back to normal, huh?"

"Not even," Scout replied. "The energies have amalgamated."

"Does this mean there is a greater chance they will become a couple?"

"That is how Rochelle and Toren's relationship started. They were friends who developed deeper feelings for one another. When an accident occurred, and they had to heal one another like April and Force did this morning, their energies mixed and their love blossomed."

"You sound displeased by this development."

"Why should I be? They'd make a perfect couple."

Scout flew to the bag with the gloves. "I'll start with these, why don't you fill the feet."

"Okay," Briella flew to a different bag and pulled out a toe sock. "Wow, they are a good colour, aren't they? He's going to be a handsomely tanned scarecrow by the time we are finished with him."

Scout's mouth rose slightly at the corners. Briella was showing signs that she was warming up to the idea of assembling a scarecrow.

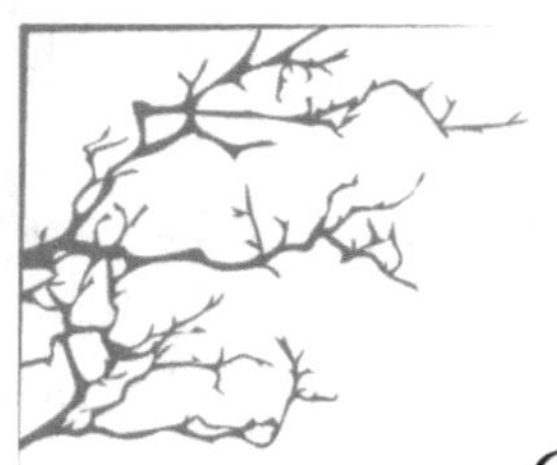

Chapter Eleven

By the time April and Force had collected enough cornstalks to fill the hessian, Briella and Scout had completed the hands and feet. They studied the interactions between Force and April which appeared friendly and awkward free. Scout sighed with relief.

"How did you get on, girls?" Force surveyed their work. "You've done well. Not too full, not too light. It will give the fingers and toes a chance to bend and move."

"Why would they need to bend and move?" Briella squeaked.

"It will make it easier to pose him on the poles I bought this morning."

"You went shopping for poles?" Scout asked.

"What did you think I was doing?"

"We weren't sure. Catching up with some of the locals, perhaps?"

"Well, I was doing stuff for my girls."

"You are going to continue to have a life outside of us right, Liam?" April asked.

"Of course, but there are no cases at the moment."

"That is not what I meant. You are going to make friendships and seek other people's company while you are living here. You aren't going to rely on us to keep you entertained every second of the day."

"Is that what you want, April?" he returned.

"I won't be living here every second of the day. I probably won't spend more than a couple of weeks a year here."

"Who's hungry?" Everyone's eyes turned to Scout. She clasped her hands and smiled sweetly. April checked her watch and moved to the kitchen without a word. She gathered plates, glasses and cutlery.

April took some lettuce, cheese, tomato, and ham from the fridge. She collected eight slices of bread from the bread bin and a couple of small mushrooms from the bottom cupboard. In no time she had made sandwiches and poured sparkling grape juice into glasses. The fairies would be dining on mushrooms and daisies.

Their meal was taken in silence. Each lost in their own thoughts. While Force cleared away the dishes, April began stuffing the jeans. She was working on the second leg when Force picked up the t-shirt and started filling the sleeves.

The fairies sat on the bench and watched them work, swinging their legs over the side. Scout's mind soon began to wander. "Oh, Briella. We forgot to create the invitations to the party," she gasped.

Briella's hands flew to her face. "What are we going to do?"

"Well, we're not going to panic," Scout began, drawing a moan from Briella.

"This is becoming a little repetitive, Scout."

"What is?"

"Well, we're not going to panic," she replied in a mocking tone.

"Whatever," Scout shook her hands to waive the interruption away. "Go and draw a template, something creepy. I'll make copies and add names."

"It's too late for that, Scout. The party's about a week away."

"You're right. That means we have less than a week to get the word out. Okay. New plan. Make a template for display in public places; school notice board, local church, the board downstairs, etc. We can get Force and April to pin them up and go from there."

"We won't know who is coming."

"Are you kidding? It's Force and April. Everyone will come."

"You're right."

The girls flew to the studio. Their departure went unnoticed by the Gatherers who had become totally engrossed in creating the scarecrow. Briella sat at her easel and opened the sketchpad to a new page. After a few seconds of staring at the white paper, her mind began to see the finished product. She picked up her pencil and, with confident strokes, set about creating an invitation to rival all others.

Briella created the outline of a scroll across the top. Inside she wrote, '*You are invited to Halloween Hollow*'.

"Oh, that's good," Scout blurted.

"Sit quietly or help the others," she was warned.

Scout zipped her lips and held up her hands. Briella smirked then returned to her project. In the bottom-right-hand-corner, she drew a reaper with a scythe. Along the blade, she wrote the date of the party. In the bottom-left-hand-corner, she outlined a werewolf with a speech bubble, '*Come if you dare*'. Between the two pictures, she drew a line of gravestones in all shapes and sizes. On them, she wrote their new address.

The middle of the invite showcased the main attraction: The House of Horrors. '*Only the brave shall enter.*'

From the bottom of the banner to the roof of the house, Briella drew vines with jack-o-lanterns swinging from them. Once again, Scout was in awe of Briella's ability. She sprinkled some magic on the page and whispered, "Times ten."

The poster multiplied itself, stacking the copies beside the original in a neat pile.

"Thanks, Scout," Briella wrapped her arms around Scout's shoulders.

"Don't sweat it. You'll be back to using your magic soon."

April called to Briella. The fairies flew back to the living area. "Where did you two go?"

"We made the invitations for the party. Can you stick them around the town later?"

"I *can*, but I don't know if I *will*," April huffed.

"Don't be a nasty woman, April," Briella scowled. "And stop correcting my grammar."

April and Force shared a thought behind their smiles that couldn't be read by the fairies. Scout narrowed her eyes and pursed her lips.

"We'll take care of it later, I promise," April replied. "Now about the scarecrow. Where do you want his eyes and mouth?"

Briella looked at the plumped out cushion of hessian. She pointed to the spots she wanted to be cut then held her breath. The holes appeared, one by one. Her breathing became more ragged with each snip of the scissors. By the time April had finished, Briella was almost on the verge of hyperventilating. Scout grabbed her by the back of the neck and forced her head between her legs.

"Deep breaths, Briella. Nice and slow. Good girl."

"I'm sorry, Scout. I don't know what came over me," Briella stated, lifting herself slightly.

"The scarecrow is becoming more real with human-like features," Scout replied. "In the bag of goodies that April brought home, I saw some orange eyes used by doll makers to create large teddy bears, and a pair of lips like those found on Mr Potato Head. Do you think that will make it harder or easier to look at him?"

"It's gotta be easier than looking at holes with bits of plant poking out, don't you think?"

"Let's see," Scout shrugged. "Put 'em in, April," Scout encouraged.

"Righty-o," she said uncertainly, reaching for the packaging.

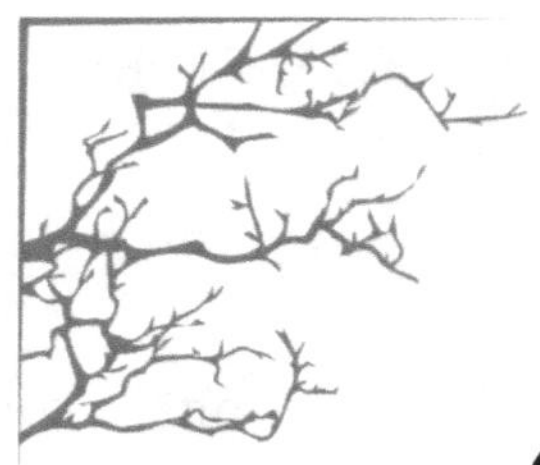

Chapter Twelve

Briella eyed the scarecrow cautiously. She wasn't sure what was worse, the eyeless pits that had been there moments ago or the dead, orange irises that now peered at her. After staring at the face for a few moments, she decided the eyes were an improvement.

The mouth, however, was laughable. It was too high. From the tips of the peaks to the outline of the bottom lip was five centimetres, at least two centimetres more than was needed. The width was too short and needed to be at least twice the size.

"Can you do something with the mouth, April? It looks weird."

"Sure," she responded, using her power over the elements to reshape the mouth so that it appeared more natural. "How's that?"

"Better. Can you change the colour? It's a bit pale, don't you think?"

"I could apply some lipstick," April mocked. The fairies burst into laughter.

"I'd bet he would be the first scarecrow in the world to have his face painted like a girl," Scout giggled.

"Not going to happen," Force's forceful voice sliced through their playfulness. "I've got some paint in the cupboard. I'm sure I can mix up a natural colour for our friend here."

"And spoil our fun?" April shoved his shoulder with her arm.

"I'm not letting you paint his face with makeup. How's he gonna be a manly scarecrow, protecting the paddocks from the birds when he's got that stuff plastered all over his face?"

"He's not real, Force. He wouldn't know the difference. Why are you making such a big deal out of this?"

"I'm not. You are," he answered, opening the door.

"Where are you going?"

He looked at her incredulously, "To get the paint."

April glanced at the fairies. They seemed as miffed as she was by his reaction.

"Well, that was strange," April said. "Is there anything you want to change, Briella?"

"Put his hat on. He looks funny bald."

April secured the straw hat to his head by tightening the cords beneath his chin. Briella eyed them uncertainly. "Do you think they look a bit girly?"

"What?" April asked.

"The cords. Do you think a guy would wear his hat like that?"

"Hmmm, you could be right," she said, taking in his appearance. "But it's not like he can hold his hat on in the midst of a gust of wind. His hat will fly off and he'll be bald again. The hessian holding his innards will be more susceptible to the elements."

"How long are we going to keep him?" Briella asked.

"As long as he lasts," April shrugged. "No point in pulling him apart again."

"I guess," Briella replied.

"Why don't you come closer?" Scout suggested, intrigued by the movement of the needle and thread as April attached an arm to the sleeve of the t-shirt.

"I don't know," Briella shook her head.

"You'll be right," Scout said softly, poking the scarecrow in the face. "See?"

Briella waited for the scarecrow to retaliate. She knew deep down that wasn't going to happen and yet, part of her was absolutely terrified that somehow the scarecrow would hurt her friend. After a few minutes, she had to admit her fear was unfounded. She flew closer to their creation and fluttered at chest height. "Touch him," Scout encouraged.

Briella shook her head. "That's a negative," she stated.

Scout poked him again. "He's amazingly squishy," she sang. Briella glanced away, ashamed of her inability to touch the thing. Scout flew to her friend and gently gripped her by the arm.

She led her down until they were millimetres from the denim. "Just a little more and you will be touching him with your feet. Your wings are free, you can escape whenever you want."

Briella stared at her friend and with a complete leap of faith, allowed the soles of her feet to touch the material. Even though she barely weighed more than a AA battery, her landing made a slight depression in his leg. "He *is* squishy," Briella cried, bouncing on the spot. "This feels awesome." Her squeal of delight brought a relieved smile to their lips.

Force wandered in with some paint on a plate. "What do you think of this colour?" His eyes widened as they observed Briella's behaviour. She flew over to contemplate the colour. "That should be perfect for his skin tone and the clothes he is wearing," she nodded.

"I see somebody is acting like their usual self," he responded to her comment.

Briella appeared shocked. "Why, whatever do you mean?" His flustered attempt at defending himself had her howling with laughter. "You know, you could do with a makeover yourself," she eyed him critically.

"Don't even start," he warned with narrowed eyes. "I'm quite comfortable with what I'm wearing." Briella liked the pale grey t-shirt and blue jeans he had put on that morning. He had even remembered to portray his eyes as milk chocolate coloured.

"I just thought you might like to wear your official uniform when you pin up the Halloween fliers."

"Why would I need to do that?"

"It makes your butt look good."

"That's not sexist at all," Force replied sarcastically. "Surely, I don't need to dress *'in a certain way'* to have people attend our Halloween party."

"Of course not," Scout answered on behalf of Briella. "Though it doesn't hurt. You haven't given the ladies anything exciting to look at for a few days."

"There are plenty of good-looking fellows in town for the ladies to go gaga over. Besides, I'm not looking for a relationship."

"Does Loretta know that?" Scout scowled.

"Loretta and I are just friends. How many times do I need to tell you that?"

"I think the man doth protest too much," Scout grinned.

Force rolled his eyes and turned their attention back to the paint. "So that's a yes, to the paint job?"

"Affirmative," Briella nodded.

"You'll need to wait until I've finished sewing on his appendages, or else I might get paint on my clothes."

"The paint will have dried out by then," Force whined.

"You can rehydrate it in an instant," April reminded him.

"That's beside the point. I went to a lot of trouble to get the tone right."

"And yet, the shade of lipstick in my bag would have been perfect. No effort spent."

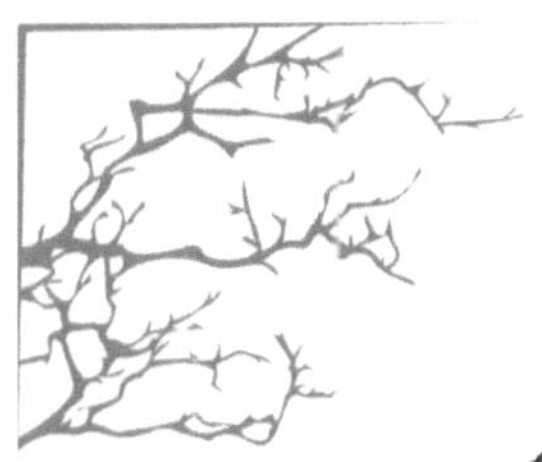

Chapter Thirteen

The girls were quite bored by the time April finished sewing the scarecrow together and Force applied the lip colour. Briella eyed their creation in awe. His eyes were disturbing. She was sure he would do a great job scaring away the birds.

"We should put him out in the field," she blurted out.

"Been doing some deep thinking?" Force asked.

"Yeah. Although I'm not particularly scared of this one, I'm not partial to coming across him in the middle of the night, perched there on the lounge chair, either. I think he would be happier hanging out in the vegetable patch."

"Okay," Force said. "Where exactly would you like to put him? I'll grab the poles and prepare his resting place."

"Oh, he won't be resting," Briella told him, fluttering in front of his face. "He'll be working hard, scaring the birds away."

Force peered over at April. She shook her head ever so slightly, afraid Briella might see. Force nodded his head, understanding completely. Briella had no idea how Scarecrows worked. She didn't seem to realise they didn't do any work at all. They simply hung on the pole. The way the birds avoided the scarecrow was actually quite fascinating, now that Force thought about it. Why were they scared of something that didn't move?

"Force, are you listening to me?" He blinked his eyes and concentrated on Briella's face.

"I'm sorry, love. What did you say?" he replied, noticing the corners of April's mouth drop. Frowning deeply, he tried to keep his focus on Briella, rather than letting his mind worry over April's reaction.

"I asked if I could come with you," Briella grumbled.

"Sure. We can all go. It will be like a family outing," he said, his face smoothing out.

April's eyebrows furrowed, and her mouth twisted slightly to the right. *'What is she thinking?'* he wondered, annoyed she had blocked him from connecting with her through mind-link. He mulled over the past few minutes and came to a conclusion. April liked him more than she was letting on.

April glanced up to see the boyish grin on his face. He heard her heartbeat quicken and turned his head away to avoid her seeing the way her reaction had affected him. *'Finally,'* he sighed. She had unwittingly given him permission to pursue a relationship with her. He would have to take it slowly. She was like a small bird. Move too fast, and she would fly away in fright.

"Who's ready?" he said, voice rising high with excitement.

"Me," Briella and Scout called out.

April kept her eyes low, placing the pins, needle and remaining thread securely in her sewing kit.

"Are you coming, April?" Force asked quietly.

"Sure, why not?" she answered, meeting his eyes but wishing she hadn't. Something was glimmering in them that she couldn't read. It made her feel nervous. "I just need to grab my hat and shoes."

Force lifted the scarecrow, and threw him over his shoulder as he headed for the door. April grabbed a white bucket hat off a hook by the door and slid her feet into a pair of navy blue slip-ons. Briella said, "Now that's what I'm talking about."

Force spun around, nearly knocking the fairies with the scarecrow. Briella pointed to April, "Her shoes match her short-sleeved top while her hat matches her jeans. Co-ordinated outfits are more appealing than clothes that are slapped on without thought." Force grumped out an answer that nobody wanted to hear. "Such language," Briella scolded.

He stormed out of the room and down the stairs. Briella and Scout flew quietly behind him. "Why do you and April always have to put him in a bad mood?" Scout enquired.

"We don't," Briella denied.

"Yes, you do," Scout returned. "There hasn't been a day since you started living here; well, except for the first couple, that one of you hasn't upset him."

Briella considered her words. "I guess we are not used to being in each other's pocket, twenty-four-seven. Maybe this isn't going to work out after all."

"Don't say that. I'm sure if we are aware of the effect we are having on one another, we can fix it."

"Maybe."

"You don't seem too sure about that," Scout muttered.

"I'm not. I think I might have been more excited by the *thought* of living with you occasionally, than actually doing it. I left Fairyland for a reason. Besides the fact I am exceptionally skilled at locating monsters, I am not that great at being around other fairies. I'm sorry to say this, Scout, but even ones I love as much as you."

Scout breathed a sigh of relief. "Oh my God, Briella. I feel exactly the same way. I didn't know how to tell you that having you here all the time is beginning to get on my nerves."

Briella flew closer to Scout, grasping her by the hand. "We must keep our communication honest, Scout. Your friendship is too important to me, for me to let the fear of hurting your feelings ultimately drive a wedge between us."

"Same here. I don't know how I feel about Force," Scout confessed. "I have loved him for a long time, but I don't know if that is as a friend or something more substantial."

"But he's a Gatherer, Scout. You're a fairy. How would that work?"

"I don't know. I am happy that April and Force have a deep connection with each other, but I am also fiercely jealous. I am so confused. I love April and hate her at the same time. What does that say about me?"

"That your feelings are typical of a person who loves people deeply. It will sort itself out. Whatever is meant to be will come to pass. Although, I must say, us being truthful with one another and everything, I couldn't see Force spending his time as a little person to be able to have a relationship with you, and you can't make yourself big."

"I know," Scout's voice almost broke over the words.

"The latest word on the fairy vine is that Queen Glitter is organising another ball. Maybe we should go together this year. That way, I might actually get to see what really goes on behind closed doors," Briella smirked.

"You'll need to wear something appropriate," Scout reminded her.

"I know. It will be nice to wear a beautiful ball gown for someone other than April."

"Ball gown?" Scout gulped.

"How is it that Queen Glitter lets you stay if you aren't wearing a ball gown?" Briella frowned.

"I don't attend them as a guest, Briella. I'm there as the help, serving food and drinks."

Briella rubbed her hands together, "You are definitely coming to the next ball with me, as a guest. We are going to have so much fun together.

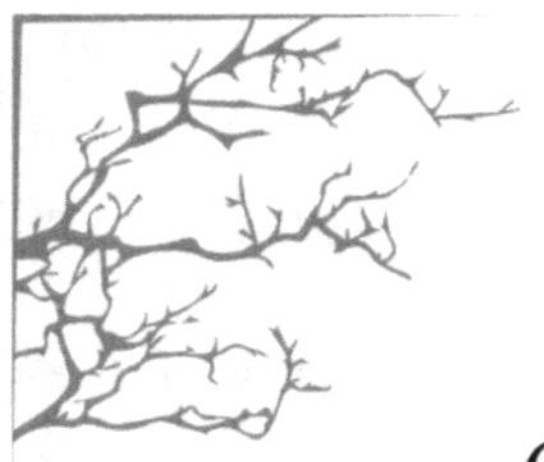

Chapter Fourteen

The team arrived at the cornfield. Briella picked out a place for her new scarecrow to reside. Force shifted the earth aside, providing a deep hole for the supporting pole to rest in. He slid it into place and then compacted the dirt tightly around the base.

April raised the other pole so that it lay horizontally on the bar. She used her powers to meld the two pieces of metal, then watched as Force wrapped the arms of the scarecrow around the rod, allowing his feet to fall.

"That doesn't look comfortable," Briella murmured, imagining herself hanging there.

"He can't feel anything, Briella," Force said.

"That doesn't matter. He is going to be hanging there a long time. Maybe the weight of his body will rip his arms from his body if we don't put some kind of support beneath his feet."

Force stared at her for what seemed like minutes but was probably just a few seconds. He transformed himself into a red and white husky then ran back to the pub. He arrived back at the cornfield shortly after with a piece of flat metal. Morphing back to his human form, Force untied the sheet from his midsection and placed it against the supporting pole. With a bit of heat, it too was fused together.

Force grabbed the feet of the scarecrow and placed them carefully on the platform. He manoeuvred the scarecrow until it rested securely on its post. "Mr Scarecrow, ready for duty," he stated, snapping to attention and saluting the guard.

Briella expected the scarecrow to return the salute and found herself feeling disappointed when he didn't. "It is so weird, I keep expecting him to act like a real person."

"Maybe subconsciously, you want him to be," Scout suggested. "You could sprinkle him with some fairy dust and test out our theory."

"What theory would that be?" Force inquired.

"That non-living things that are sprinkled with Briella's fairy dust, which ultimately come to life, can be controlled by her."

"When did you come up with that theory?" April asked.

"While I was in the House of Horrors. The creatures that came to life from my drawings were bound to do whatever I commanded them to do," Briella said with embarrassment.

"So, you think that if you were to bring the scarecrow to life with your wayward magic, he would have to do what you say?"

"That's the theory. I'm not sure Briella is ready to test it though," Scout said, looking at her friend. A quick shake of the head confirmed Scout's thoughts. "I didn't think so. You've made heaps of progress with your magical issue, Briella. It is probably a good thing not to push the boundaries too far."

"I agree," April said, "especially considering the fact that you have kept it a secret for centuries."

"Next year will be different again," Briella reminded her. "We won't be facing the same issues that are occurring this year."

"I know. But, we will face whatever comes, *together*," April replied.

Briella nodded and fluttered up to the scarecrow's face. She viewed him sadly. "I don't know why I was ever scared of you. You are quite pathetic actually, hanging there for your entire lifespan. Whatever that may be." She landed on his shoulder and gazed out over the meadow. "I might just stay here for a while."

"Do you want some company?" Scout inquired.

"Nah. Some time alone will do me a world of good."

"I might head into the woods for a couple of hours if that's okay with you two?" Scout glanced over at April and Force.

"Fine by me," Force stated.

"I got some things to take care of. I'll see you all later," April stated, heading towards the pub.

"Where are you headed?" Force asked curiously.

"I need to return something we didn't need," she answered.

"What is it? Maybe I could use it for another project."

"I don't think so," April said with a secret smile.

"Can I walk back with you?"

"Of course. What are your plans for the rest of the day?"

"Callum and I have an appointment."

"You're working a job?"

"We have to convince people that you have a husband and I have a twin brother."

"Oh, right."

Their voices faded to nothing as they wandered back to the pub. Briella took note of their body language. They were relaxed and seemed to be enjoying one another's company. Briella wondered how long that would last. Would April have upset Force in some way before they reached the building? More than likely.

She thought about the relationship that existed between the four of them. There was no way they would be able to make this holiday thing work. Briella realised how she had started to lose part of herself living with Scout. With each passing day, she was beginning to take on some of Scout's mannerisms and thought patterns. She also saw how Scout had changed in the few days they had been living together.

While Briella had wanted her to become more comfortable with change, she realised Scout was becoming a different person altogether. If they became too much like one another, would they still get on or would they start disliking one another?

"Oh, I've made a terrible mistake," she told the scarecrow. "I've always loved Scout, just the way she is. Why would I want to change her?" There was no answer forthcoming. "You're no help," she swung her legs and kicked him.

"Would you behave yourself if I sprinkled some dust on you?" she asked the scarecrow, looking up at his face. His eyes stared vacantly across the field. A couple of crows circled cautiously above. They cawed to one another with annoyance that the humans would be so cruel as to place a scarecrow near their corn. "Should I risk it? What is the worst that could happen?" Briella tapped a finger against her chin.

"The humans could discover the existence of magic. The Gatherers would need to wipe their memories before they were able to share their discovery with the world. No big deal. She stood on his shoulder and tapped her foot. "Of course, there was the dream. You chasing me through the cornfield, threatening my life. Was that my fear manifesting itself in my dreams, or was it a vision, a prophecy of what is to come?"

Briella didn't know what to do. She wanted somebody to talk to. Someone she could discuss her issues with. She couldn't very well tell Scout, April or Force. Other than the Locator Fairies, no-one knew of her existence. The nearest fairy was too far away to get to before nightfall, not that she wanted them to know her business anyway. Her best shot at getting things straight in her head was to bring the scarecrow to life and talk to him. But would he listen to her, and would he be smart enough to have the right answers? She could sprinkle her dust and find he doesn't have the answers and that he is not under her control like she hoped.

Briella breathed deeply. "Life is supposed to be lived, not worried over." She sprinkled some dust then held her breath.

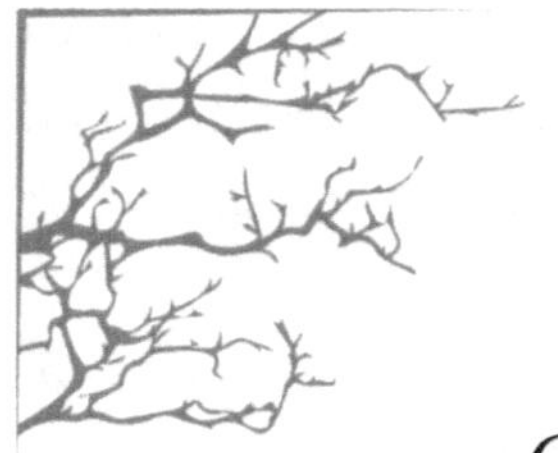

Chapter Fifteen

The scarecrow twitched. His body produced small shudders that gradually grew to the point where Briella had to fly away or be thrown off. His eyes blinked numerous times while they acclimatised themselves to the sunlight. His mouth opened and closed continuously, while his throat worked furiously to create sound.

The legs were so restless they came off the support ledge while his arms jerked wildly, trying to tear himself free of his restraints. Briella was afraid he would injure himself and flew in to offer assistance. "You need to unhook your arms from the pole before trying to raise them!" she yelled.

The scarecrow looked at her blankly, not comprehending her words. She turned around and spread her arms out like his. Then she showed him the motion required that would unhook his arms. He copied, raising them and lifting himself off. With a terrible thud, he fell to the ground, smacking his head and crushing his hat beneath him. "Ooof," the air was pushed from his torso.

"Are you okay?" Briella asked, hovering above him.

The scarecrow rolled onto his back and gazed at the sky. He blinked several times before raising himself into a seated position. "Bright," he said.

"Yes, the sun is dangerous. You shouldn't look into it directly."

"Why am I here?"

"I created you," Briella admitted while wringing her hands.

"Why?" his attention soon turning to the circling birds above. "Birds," he snarled launching to his feet and flapping his arms in the air. The birds squawked as they flew south, the scarecrow in hot pursuit.

"Wait!" Briella cried. He stopped in his tracks and turned to face her.

"What?" he asked, dancing on his feet. He was itching to continue the chase.

"You mustn't leave this area," she said.

"What area?"

She glanced around and saw that there weren't enough objects to use to define the boundaries for him. "Do you understand distance?" she queried.

"Distance?"

"Ooh," she growled, fluttering up and down. "You must keep the birds away from the food. Especially the corn. If you go too far from the cornstalks, they will be able to pick at the kernels."

"They are not to eat the corn," the scarecrow agreed. He ran back to the cornfield and ran around the perimeter. "No birds," he stated.

"No birds," she agreed. "They will come back."

"I will be waiting," the scarecrow crossed his arms and nodded.

His eyes continuously scanned the sky, looking for his adversaries. "You don't need to be so vigilant. You will hear the flapping of their wings when they return."

"I cannot hear yours," the scarecrow said.

"I'm a lot smaller than a crow," she stated the obvious.

"Indeed. Other types of birds will come for the food."

"Yes," Briella said.

"Then I must be vigilant. They may be small like you, and I may not hear them. I must keep my eyes moving."

"I thought we might be able to talk," Briella began. "I've got some issues and could do with some advice."

"Maybe when I am finished working. I cannot be distracted from my duties," he said.

Briella put on her sad face which did nothing to sway his opinion. "May I sit on your shoulder? I'm going to get awfully tired flapping my wings all afternoon."

"Do you not have anything better to do than to watch me work?"

"Actually, no. I told my friends I needed some time on my own."

"You are not going to have that if you stay with me," his eyes continued to scan above.

"Oh, I don't know," she landed on his shoulder. "You can be with someone and still be alone." She sat forlornly, slowly swinging her legs.

"That does not make sense."

Briella didn't argue with him. What was the point? He was more focused on chasing away the birds than holding a conversation with her. Actually, it was more than not wanting to talk to her. He didn't really have any interest in her at all. "Do you have a name?"

"Why would I need one?" he answered.

"Everybody has a name," Briella said. The scarecrow said nothing. He continued to look for birds to chase. "I would have been better off with a dog," she muttered. "Way more loyal, although, he probably would have tried to eat me by now. Of course, I might have been able to control him and told him not to eat me. But then maybe he wouldn't have listened and eaten me anyway. Oh, my goodness. What has my life come to? I need to get back to my normal routine. I need to go back to our apartment."

Briella felt a weight lifting from her shoulders. Two revelations in one day. It had to be a world record for her. She considered leaving the scarecrow but wasn't sure if he would stay near the cornfields. Just because he had so far, didn't mean that would continue. She wasn't sure if he was doing what he was told, or afraid the birds would get the corn.

What if a bird was to fly near the pumpkin patch, or over by the tomatoes, cucumbers and cauliflowers? Would he chase them over there and then continue onto the watermelons, pineapples and grapes the neighbours were growing? She would have to stay and ensure he remained unnoticed by the humans.

She could always tell him to strike a pose should a human wander into view. Of course, she had no way of knowing if he would follow her command without it being tested. Briella searched the area. There was nobody in sight to test him with. "Do you want to play a game?" she asked him.

"Working," he replied.

"It will help you scare the birds," she lied.

"Sure, what do I have to do?"

"Stand as still as you can in a freaky pose."

He eyed her strangely. "That is ridiculous. Why don't you go find something else to do? Like I said to you before, I have a job to do."

Briella flew to the edge of the forest and sat on a rock. She grabbed a small mushroom from the base and began to chew. "I should have asked Scout to stay."

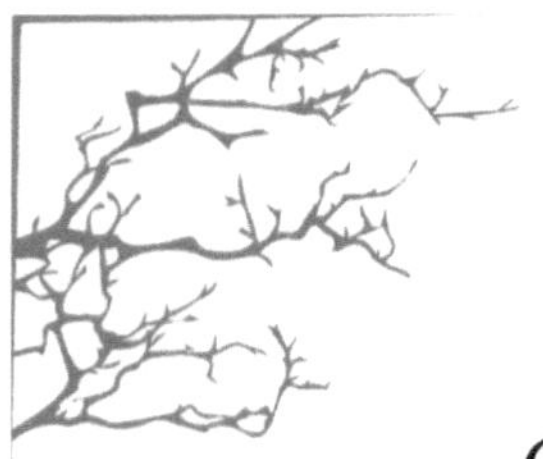

Chapter Sixteen

Briella was bored out of her brains. She wished she hadn't brought the scarecrow to life. Her favourite show would be coming on television soon, and now because of the scarecrow, she was going to miss it.

Briella paced along the top of the rock. She had to watch where she put her feet due to the uneven edges. Pretty soon her neck was beginning to hurt. "God, if I'm this bored now, what is night time going to be like?"

She heard them before she saw them. A murder of crows was racing towards the cornfield. Briella raised her head and watched their advance. "I'll be damned." Her eyes were curious, her mind racing as she tried to work out what was going on. Her brain came up with the bright idea that the earlier crows had come back with reinforcements.

Briella placed her hands on her hips. Her eyes were rooted to the sky. She turned her head so that the scarecrow came into view. He was standing no more than twenty metres from the edge of the cornfield. His stance was aggressive as he prepared himself for their onslaught.

At first, they did nothing, continuing to circle ominously above. Briella smiled. They were scared of him. She had done well in her selection of materials for his construction. The corn would be safe, and the scarecrow would have something to keep him occupied until nightfall. Briella glanced towards the woods. She wondered what Scout was doing and thought it a shame that Scout would not get to witness the scarecrow's first success.

The birds cawed to one another. More coming to join them until the group consisted of more than one hundred. There were enough bodies in the air to cast a shadow over the cornfield below. Briella's stomach began to twist, the mushroom no longer sitting so well inside. Her mouth began to water, and she swallowed uncomfortably. She glanced at the scarecrow with worried eyes.

He eyed the birds with concern. There were so many of them. He had expected to chase the odd bird or two. Not an army of them. He watched their flight patterns, trying to discern their plan. As the first of the birds began their bomb dive, he threw his hat to the side and flexed his non-existent muscles. "You should have given me more padding, fairy," he yelled, never taking his eyes off the birds.

Briella had to admit he was right. He looked like a skinny weed about to be cut into threads by a line of lawn mowers. "You'll be all right," she yelled, not knowing if he could hear her. The monsters in the House of Horrors had been able to understand her through mind-link. Would it work the same for something created out of man-made objects?

The first of the birds reached the scarecrow, his arms coming up to pluck them from the sky. They changed direction at the last minute, staying just out of reach, before beginning their climb. The next line of attackers swooped, one of them managing to get its beak into the back of his head. "Don't worry about the ones that have passed," Briella shrieked. "Keep your eyes on those that are still coming."

The scarecrow was turning in a circle, his arms waving madly above him. Briella worried that she hadn't given him the skills required to take on such a task. She didn't know enough about them, having been too scared to approach them in the fields. She watched in horror as the third assault began, crows approaching from all sides. "You are supposed to be afraid of him!" she shouted at them.

Her arm came up as the first bird reached him, as did the scarecrow's. His fist connected with the bird's chest, sending it spiralling through the air. "Whoop," Briella cried with excitement. A bird swooped from behind him. She lifted her back leg and threw it over her head, resulting in a forward roll. The scarecrow did the same, taking out another bird. Briella glowed with happiness. "So, we are connected, after all."

The birds circled above, wary of the creature below them. Their leader had told them tales of destroying other scarecrows in the area and laughing at the humans who put them there. None of those had ever fought back. Their leader was not about to be thwarted. To back down would mean losing his place as head bird and he couldn't have that. There was no way he was going to live out his days as an outcast.

He organised them into a circle and gave the order to attack. All of the birds descended as one. Briella gasped with horror. Her scarecrow was going to be torn to bits. There was no way he could fight them all off at once. Many of them would be able to sink their claws into his clothes, ripping them, allowing the birds to use their beaks to tear him apart.

Briella's wings flapped furiously. She had to help him somehow, but if she flew into the middle of their onslaught, she could very well die herself. Briella searched in vain for something that would even the odds. She realised the only things she could do was to show pride for her creation and bear witness to his end.

Her hands flew to her cheeks as she screamed in pain. As the birds neared, she wrapped her arms around her midriff and braced herself for what was to come. What happened next was something she would remember for all time.

It was like a scene out of a Jackie Chan movie. Legs and arms were everywhere, his body spinning and twisting through the air. Birds were flying in all directions, and not of their own accord. The scarecrow was kicking feathers and holding his own. He was a force to be reckoned with, and the reckoning was being held that minute.

Briella's eyes widened in surprise. She couldn't believe what she was seeing. He was an organic machine of epic proportions, and he was there because of her. "I created him," she said in awe, unable to believe she was capable of making something so wonderful. "This cannot be so," she muttered.

Injured birds littered the ground. The remaining birds took off in fear, never to return. The scarecrow moved from one bird to the next, tending to their wounds. He spoke quietly, yet firmly, instilling in them the desire to stay away from the fairy's garden. The birds that were able to fly left. Those that couldn't, would be treated by April or Force as soon as Briella located one of them.

She fluttered in front of the scarecrow's face. "You were amazing," she said quietly. "How did you do it?"

"Instinct," he replied sadly. "I did not want to hurt them, but they left me with no choice."

"I don't think you'll have that problem again."

"You don't think they will come back with a bigger army?"

"No," Briella shook her head. "I think they are passing on the news of the fierce scarecrow they encountered in this cornfield and warning other birds to stay away from here, if they value their lives. You have just become a legend. I think they will venture somewhere else for their dining needs. A place that is not guarded by a scarecrow. Birds, like any other creature, are interested in the easiest way to secure their food. You were so brave."

"I was doing what you created me to do."

"That was above and beyond the scope of your job, don't you think?"

"No, I do not. You wanted me to keep the birds away from the corn, and that is what I did."

"Thank you, Mr Scarecrow. I appreciate your service."

"You are welcome. I think I had better get some help for these birds. They appear to have broken wings."

"I'll get help. You stay here and watch over them."

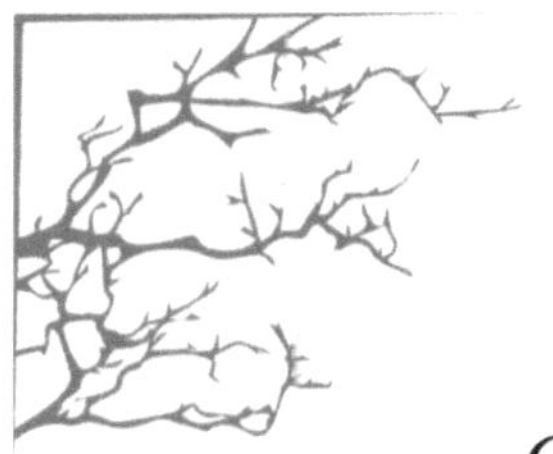

Chapter Seventeen

Briella found Force, who dropped everything, returned quickly, and healed the injured birds. After hearing of the battle between the scarecrow and the birds, he wished Briella had not sent him away. "I would have liked to have seen that," he stated.

"Yes, but if you had been here, you might have helped, and it wouldn't have been as spectacular."

"True that," Force replied. "Pity you didn't capture it on camera."

"How would I do that?"

"With a mobile phone. They have fantastic cameras in them these days."

"April is going to get me one soon. You'll have to teach me how to use it."

"That would be my pleasure. 'Though, wouldn't it be easier for you to learn from April?"

"I've never seen her take pictures. I've only seen her use it to talk to people."

Force looked at the scarecrow who had taken to watching the sky again. Briella saw that he was going to say something and stopped him. "If you are going to tell him to relax, don't bother. It seems that this one is better than any guard dog I've ever come across. He takes his job seriously and refuses to stand down."

"What is he going to do when it gets dark?"

"I guess he will guard the corn against the fruit bats."

"But they don't eat corn."

"*We* know that. He will be inanimate come sunrise."

"I know," Force said. "Until then, what do we do with him?"

"Leave him to it, I guess. He is the most boring person, ever. He won't make eye contact when he talks and only has half his mind on the conversation. The other half is persistently looking for birds."

"You sound disappointed."

"I am," she laughed. "I was so scared of him when he was a figment of my imagination. When we created him for real, I was still a little afraid of him. Now I am miffed that I cannot hold his attention. He brushes me aside as though I am not important. I don't like feeling insignificant."

"You will never be insignificant, Briella. You are instrumental in keeping the humans safe from creatures that would do them harm. You will always be important."

"Thanks, Force. Do you know what it was that April had to return?"

"No, I don't know," he lied. He had seen the package when she had retrieved it from the drawer and tried to sneak it into her bag. He was pretty sure she had bought some pretty underwear when she had been under the influence of the energy transfer. Since their energy had returned to normal, she probably felt uncomfortable with the fact she had wanted him to kiss her, and decided to return the items. Force wasn't concerned. She looked beautiful even when she wasn't wearing pretty underwear that increased her confidence.

"What do you want to do now?"

"I don't know. Do you want to watch *'How Do I Look?'* on the television?"

He didn't, but caught the hint that she wanted some company. As April was still in town and Scout was off doing her own thing, he said, "That would be great. Do we need to pick up some snacks?"

"No, that won't be necessary. Do you think we could make a second scarecrow?"

"You want another one?"

"Not for me. For him," she pointed in his direction. "Don't you think it would be nice to have a female scarecrow to keep him company in the garden?"

"He won't be conscious to realise he has a partner."

"I know. But I'll know there is a friend out there for him, and it will make me feel better."

Force hadn't realised how deep Briella's heart ran. "That is a beautiful thing," he admitted, thinking how lonely it would be out here day after day. "Are you going to give them an opportunity to get to know one another before sunrise?"

"Nah. That would complicate things for Mr Scarecrow. Look how happy he is standing guard. I couldn't take that away from him."

"Are you going to bring him back to life for the party?"

"I don't know. What would be the point?"

"There wouldn't be one, I guess." Force began walking back to the pub, Briella flying beside him.

"Goodbye, Mr Scarecrow," she called over her shoulder.

"Goodbye, Fairy," he replied with a salute. "I shall continue to guard the corn with my life."

Briella felt sad. "I wish I had never let the girls talk me into making him."

"You were so scared of scarecrows, Briella, that it was affecting you in your sleep. They had to do something to keep you healthy."

"Yeah, but I feel so bad for him."

"Why? Even when he loses the magic that keeps him alive, he will be hanging on the poles, doing what he loves. A lot of people go through life, Briella, feeling as though they don't have a purpose. He is one of the luckier ones. He knows why he has been put on this Earth, and he loves what he does. You shouldn't waste your sorrow on him."

"I never thought about it that way, Force. We have a purpose in life, and it is a good one."

"It sure is," he grinned. "Speaking of purposes, there is another that I wish to push to the forefront."

"What is it?" Briella asked intrigued.

"How would you feel about me pursuing a relationship with April?"

Briella grinned, "I think that would be wonderful, but you might want to check with Scout."

"Doesn't she like April?"

"She loves April. You have worked with Scout for a very long time and you have become very close. You might want to get her blessing before you begin your quest to conquer April's heart."

"Conquer April's heart? Have you been reading some of those romance books?"

"No, I'm just a sucker for a guy who has a difficult job ahead of him."

"So, April doesn't feel anything for me?"

"On the contrary, Force. April likes you more than she wants to admit. She is scared of messing up your friendship."

"I see. Well, I'll just have to allay those fears, won't I? I think I'll begin while we're creating a girlfriend for your scarecrow."

"As long as you talk to Scout first," Briella reminded him.

They'd reached the pub and smiled as April came around the corner. She had a perplexed look on her face. "Everything all right, April?" Force inquired.

Force's words rushed through her head, although she managed to keep her face blank. She wanted to tell him he should keep his thoughts protected from mind-link, but said nothing. If he had been unguarded, she wouldn't have known he still wanted to pursue a relationship with her. She wasn't ready for that.

She knew she wouldn't be able to protect her heart from getting hurt. She already liked him more than she should. He was a colleague, and it should remain that way. April had to get away. She knew that if he kissed her, it would be all over. There would be no coming back from that.

So she said the only thing she could think of, "I've got to get back to the coast. There is a problem with one of the units that I need to take care of."

"I'll come with you," he said.

"No," she replied a little too quickly. "There's no need. It should only take a couple of days. I'll be back in time for settlement on the property."

Liam forced a fake smile, "Okay then. See you in a couple of days."

He walked inside, allowing the door to close behind him. His emotions were in too much of a turmoil to think of behaving like a gentleman. He felt like he had been kicked in the guts. As much as he tried, he couldn't shake the feeling that April was trying to distance herself from him. No amount of self-talk could shake him out of his funk. It wasn't as though she knew of his plans, and when you were a property owner, things were going to go wrong from time to time. It wasn't her fault that it happened to fall at the wrong time.

He went to his room and closed the door. April wasn't to blame, but he was still mad at her. At least he would be over these feelings by the time she returned, and he would have a new plan to break down the walls she had erected against him.

Force walked to the bedside table and opened the drawer. He grabbed a small jewellery case he'd hidden beneath some junk he kept in there. Opening the lid, his gaze fell upon a silver chain with a sapphire secured in the middle of a heart-shaped pendant. He closed his eyes and pictured the necklace nestled against April's skin.

With a smile on his face, he lowered himself until he was sitting on top of the mattress. Opening his eyes, he closed the lid and hid the case once more. Feeling a lot calmer, he walked to the window and stared into the distance.

His brain sent him an image of carrying April over the threshold of their new home. The same idea the fairies had come up with, popped into his mind. He would play the part of Wade, while Callum would be relegated to the role of playing Liam. A grin slowly spread across his face. It was time he had a talk with Scout.

Titles by Marnie Atwell

Starlight Investigations

Jealousy Monsters

Vampire

Halloween Madness

The Pumpkin Patch

The House of Horrors

The Spirited Scarecrow

About the Author

Marnie is an Australian author who lives in South-East Queensland with her husband and two children. When she is not dreaming up new adventures for her characters; Marnie enjoys writing, reading paranormal romance novels, and spending time with her family and friends. Not necessarily in that order.

Visit her website at: www.marnieatwell.com for more books, pictures, and downloads.

The next book in the Halloween Madness series is:
The Curious Kitten

www.ingramcontent.com/pod-product-compliance
Lightning Source LLC
Chambersburg PA
CBHW030437120726
47903CB00003B/1005